# HOMICIDE AT THE HARBOR

## A MADDIE MILLS COZY MYSTERY

## CINDY BELL

ISBN: 9798351955353

# CHAPTER 1

$\mathcal{M}$addie Mills reached for the coffeepot. Her outstretched fingers had almost closed around the handle, when a scraping sound emanating from the dining room made her freeze. She tilted her head to the side and listened as the sound continued. Could it be a rat? She'd caught a squirrel trying to gnaw through the roof just the day before.

The house she'd grown up in had certainly accumulated some unique guests during the years that it sat empty. Abandoning the idea of coffee for the moment, she stepped through the archway of the kitchen and into the larger space of the dining room. Her two West Highland White Terriers followed after her into the room.

"Tammy, what are you doing?" She gasped at the sight of the shredded wallpaper scattered all over the scuffed and scraped wood floors. Her sister, adorned in pink leggings and an oversized, yellow sweatshirt, stood atop a stepladder in the middle of the mess.

"It's about time this old stuff came down, don't you think?" Tammy Webber cast a wide smile over her shoulder as she teetered on the stepladder. "I was thinking we should use something bright in here, since there's only that one measly window. Maybe yellow?" She pointed to her shirt. "This is a nice shade, don't you think?"

Maddie's lips tightened. She counted to ten in her mind. Ever since her younger sister's arrival a couple of days ago, she'd been challenged by her incessant creativity, and what seemed like boundless energy.

"I thought it was fine the way it was, Tammy. Dean is going to be here any minute, and now look at this mess!" Maddie gritted her teeth. The counting didn't seem to be working.

"Oh, Dean won't mind. He'll probably want to help." Tammy grinned as she climbed down from the stepladder. "He's always been such a helpful kid. You've done such a great job with him."

"I'm not sure I can take credit for it, but yes, he is a great person. He's not coming here to work, though, Tammy. He's coming here for a brief break before his new job starts." Maddie pursed her lips. "And to check on me, I'm sure."

"All the more reason to show him that we have everything under control." Tammy dusted off her hands. "Maddie, just because you've moved back into Mama's house, doesn't mean that it has to look like Mama still lives here."

Maddie looked over the green-and-white wallpaper that had once covered the entire dining room. No, it wasn't her style. But it was exactly how she remembered it.

"I just needed a place to live, Tammy. I don't need it to be any particular way." Maddie placed her hands on her hips. "You should have asked me first."

"Oh, you're right. You're always right." Tammy brushed her blonde hair out of her eyes. "I wanted to surprise you. You've been through so much, and I just wanted to brighten your day. I'm sorry. I didn't mean to cause a problem."

"Tammy, it's okay." Maddie walked over to a section of the wallpaper that still clung to the faded paint beneath it. She tugged at the edge and savored the sound of the slow tear as it pulled away from the wall. "I know you meant well. It would be nice to brighten up this room a bit. I have to paint the outside, of course, but the inside is fine."

"Oh, Maddie, you have to make this place your own. It can't be a shrine to the past forever." Tammy tugged another strip of wallpaper.

"Dean is meeting us at Janet's Place." Maddie grabbed her purse from the hook by the door. "I want to get there early to make sure that we get a good table. We can walk over."

"Isn't it nice to live somewhere where you can just walk to everything?" Tammy smiled as she picked up her own purse. "I had no idea how much I would love coming back here." She gazed at her for a long moment. "Maybe it's a lucky break that you ended up back here, Maddie."

"Lucky break? Fresh start, maybe. But lucky break, I don't think so." Maddie patted the dogs' heads, then opened the door and stepped through it.

"I know you've been through a lot, but sometimes life can work out better that way, can't it? You think you're doing just fine, trudging along, but then bam! Something shows up out of the blue to rock your whole world, and when the dust settles, you end up exactly where you're meant to be." Tammy pulled the door shut before Bella and Polly could escape. "But if I ever get my hands on Craig." She balled her hands into fists and shook them in front of her face.

"Tammy, you don't have a violent bone in your body." Maddie laughed. "But you do look adorable when you're angry." She continued down the sidewalk, toward the harbor. "I still can't believe what he was up to. I mean he was seeing someone else, gambling away everything we owned, even committing fraud, and the whole time I thought we had a happy marriage."

"He did a good job of hiding everything." Tammy clucked her tongue.

"Did he?" Maddie quickened her pace, eager to get to the restaurant before Dean. "He was always busy, always had excuses for not being home. I knew something wasn't right, but I believed him when he said it was just a mistake. And now he's behind bars for fraud." She cringed. "I'm just glad it's over. I'm never going to let that happen to me again."

Tammy quickly turned around and grabbed her sister by the shoulders. She stared hard into her eyes.

"I'll tell you what you're not going to let happen. You're not going to let that sorry excuse for a man

5

stop you from living your best life. Do you hear me, Maddie? Now is your chance to step into something wonderful and new. Don't let his betrayal stop you from enjoying that!"

"Okay, no need for the dramatics." Maddie rolled her eyes as she smiled.

"Plenty of need." Tammy wrapped her arm around Maddie's shoulders as they strolled along the harbor, past the marina. The subtle sound of the boats rocking in the water mingled with the traffic that rolled slowly past as they made their way to the restaurant.

Maddie held open the restaurant door for Tammy to step through.

# CHAPTER 2

"*D*ean!" Tammy shrieked as she entered the restaurant.

"Hi, Aunt Tammy." Dean smiled as he stood up from a table. Even at six feet tall, with a scruffy, brown beard, and blue eyes as bright as his mother's, his eyes lit up at the sight of his mother. "Mom!"

Tammy stepped aside as Maddie rushed toward her son.

"Oh, Dean, I wanted to be here before you arrived." Maddie wrapped her arms around him in a tight hug and kissed his cheek. "It's so good to see you."

"You too, Mom." Dean smiled as he held her close. "My plane got in a bit early, so I thought I'd do a little exploring. I used to love visiting this place when I was young."

"You were always running off and trying to find some creature to bring home and terrify your grandmother with." Maddie laughed.

"Or his aunt." Tammy took her turn to hug Dean. "Wow, how do you get more handsome every time I see you?"

"I'm not so sure about that." Dean chuckled.

"It's true." Maddie sat down at the table. "I want to hear about your trip. Was it okay?"

"It was the usual." Dean sat down as well and looked around the restaurant. "I visited so long ago, but from what I remember, not much has changed around here."

"It's about to." Maddie smiled as Lacy, a young waitress, walked over. "Now that there's a new scenic route through town, they're making a lot of changes. They're building an amusement park, and lots of new buildings are going up all the time."

"That's for sure." Lacy set down menus in front of each of them. "There's so much to do at the marina now, too. Have you taken Captain Sam Niles' boat tour, yet?"

"No. Is it a gimmick or worth the time?" Maddie glanced through the large glass window in the direction of the marina. Many of the big boats had begun offering some kind of seafaring tour.

"Oh, trust me, it's worth it. He makes it an adventure. He has one starting in about an hour, if you want to go." Lacy gazed at the clock, then pulled out her order pad. "What can I get for you?"

One by one, they placed their orders.

Despite Maddie's interest in the cheeseburger sliders, she selected a salad topped with chicken and almonds.

"Are you sure that's what you want, Mom?" Dean raised his eyebrows.

"I'm trying to be healthy. Besides, I'm sure it will be delicious." Maddie focused her thoughts on her son as she noticed the way he glanced around nervously. "Dean, are you okay?" She watched him scan the restaurant again.

"Sure, I'm fine." Dean waited for Lacy to walk away, then looked over at her. "Why don't you just move in with me, Mom? There's a spare room at my place."

"You certainly don't need your mother living with you." Maddie's voice grew stern. "I'm living here. It's going to be just fine."

"I don't like it." Dean sat back in his chair and

folded his arms across his chest. "You're hours away from any of your family, and all alone."

"She's not alone. I'm here." Tammy wiggled her fingers in a small wave. "Remember?"

"For how long?" Dean looked over at Tammy. "You're going to go back home, and she's going to be living here all by herself. What sense does that make? Mom, you shouldn't be forced into this just because Dad is a jerk."

"Don't say that." Maddie leaned forward. "He's your father."

"Mom, really?" Dean looked down at the table. "I can't believe that you would defend him after what he did to you."

"He's still your father, Dean. He has been there for you your entire life. What happens in a marriage has nothing to do with what happens between a parent and child." Maddie's tone softened.

"Of course it does." Dean looked up at her. "I just don't think it's right. Maybe I could get you an apartment near me. Would you like that?"

"I don't need you to take care of me, Dean." Maddie stared hard into his eyes. "I am perfectly capable of doing that myself. I did get a degree, work as an assistant for a private investigator, raise three children, and run my home, you know."

"Mom, of course I know that you're capable, but you shouldn't have to be alone." Dean sighed and looked up at the ceiling.

"Dean, I know it's hard to believe, since your mother and I are so very old." Tammy rolled her eyes and smiled. "But we really are doing just fine. Aren't we, Maddie?" She flashed her a smile.

"Absolutely." Maddie's cheeks heated up as she noticed the attention of the other patrons. They loved to gossip and were very nosy about the newcomers in town.

"I just want to make sure that you're okay." Dean sat back as Lacy delivered a cup of coffee to him.

"Oh, you don't have to worry too much about that. Chief Holden's been keeping an eye on her ever since he walked in." Lacy winked at Maddie, then headed back toward the kitchen.

"Who?" Dean looked over the patrons again, until his gaze settled on the man in uniform near the front counter.

"Is that Jake? Jake Holden?" Tammy gasped.

"Yes." Maddie quickly glanced over at him.

"He looks so different." Tammy's eyes widened.

"That's for sure." Maddie knew Tammy was

11

remembering the lanky teenager, who had now turned into a muscular, self-assured man.

"Jake Holden! It's me, Tammy!" Tammy waved to him.

Maddie's cheeks burned as Jake turned his attention to their table. She couldn't help but wonder how much of the argument with her son he had overheard.

"Tammy?" Jake smiled as he walked over. "I was wondering when you might show up. Just like always, wherever Maddie is, you eventually pop up."

"Of course. She's my big sister, and I love her." Tammy gave Maddie's shoulder a squeeze.

"It's good to see you again, too, Maddie." Jake nodded to her, then looked past her, at Dean.

"This is my son, Dean. Dean, this is Chief Holden. We all grew up together here in Bayview." Maddie watched as the two men shook hands.

"So, you stuck around and became chief of police, huh?" Dean smiled at him.

"Yep, I can't get away from the place." Jake glanced over at Maddie. "How's the painting coming along at the house?"

"Just fine." Maddie stirred a bit of cream into her coffee.

"Slow. Very slow." Tammy shook her head. "She's just as stubborn as she's always been."

"I am not stubborn." Maddie took a sip of her coffee.

"Oh, yes you are." Dean grinned.

"I don't think it's ever going to change." Tammy laughed.

"Maybe it shouldn't." Jake met Maddie's eyes. "It's a quality I have always admired."

Maddie smiled in response to the smile that crossed Jake's lips. "I'm sure you'll have the chance to witness plenty of it. I'm not going anywhere." She shot a stern look in Dean's direction.

"I hear you, Mom. I hear you."

"I'd better get back to work." Jake tipped his hat to Dean. "It was nice to meet you, Dean." He snuck a glance at Maddie. "I hope she goes easy on you."

"Me, too." Dean feigned a wince and laughed.

Maddie leaned across the table and gave Dean's cheek a gentle pinch.

"How could I not adore a face like that?"

"Mom!" Dean groaned and pushed her hand away.

"And those dimples." Tammy grinned as she

leaned close to Maddie. "He is my most handsome nephew, you know?"

"I'm your only nephew, Aunt Tammy." Dean dodged Tammy's attempt to ruffle his hair.

Jake chuckled as he walked away from the table.

# CHAPTER 3

"*L*acy! How much do I have to pay to get some fresh coffee around here?" a man at another table shouted across the restaurant.

Lacy hurried over to the coffeepots. "Sorry, Tim. Coming right up."

Maddie glanced over at Tim. He looked to be in his late thirties, with short, black hair. She didn't recognize him. She watched as he turned his attention back to the well-dressed man who sat across from him.

"I just want to know why there's a delay. How come every time I call you, you tell me that you need another day or so, and it turns into a week?" The man leaned forward and glared at Tim. He had chiseled features, amplified by the scowl on his face. "Can you explain that to me? Because it sure feels like you're messing me around here. I don't have an endless supply of money to keep delaying things."

"Relax, relax, Lawson." Tim smiled and scooted his chair closer. "You know, things in these small towns take forever to get done. But it's going to get done. Until then, just enjoy the view. What a beautiful place, right?" He gestured to the large window that overlooked the bay. "Get out on one of those boat trips that you love so much when you come to Bayview. Have yourself some fun. Leave the worrying to me. All right?"

"Here you go, Tim." Lacy set a cup of coffee down beside him. "Sorry it took so long."

"It's all right, Lacy." Tim slid a twenty across the table toward her. "Keep the change."

"Generous guy. Pity it doesn't make up for the fact he spoke to her badly." Maddie looked over at Dean. "When we finish here, we should check out the marina. You're going to love it."

"Here you are." Lacy set their plates down in front of them and cast a wary look in Tim and Lawson's direction.

"Maybe Lacy will tell me more." Dean met Lacy's eyes as a slow smile spread across his lips.

"How come the chief of police is keeping an eye on my mother?"

"Don't answer that, Lacy." Maddie cut her gaze sternly in the young woman's direction.

"Don't worry, I'll keep an eye on your mom, and Jake, while I'm here." Tammy grinned as she had a bite of her sandwich.

"I'm glad you'll be here for a little while." Dean glanced at his mother. "So, you'll have someone to keep an eye on you." He put a fry in his mouth.

"And what about you?" Maddie scooted her chair closer to his. "Who is going to keep an eye on you, Dean?"

Dean stared out through the front window of the restaurant and didn't respond.

"Dean?" Maddie tapped his arm lightly.

He stood up abruptly and strode across the restaurant to the front door.

"Dean? It was just a joke!" Maddie followed after him. She caught up with him as he pulled open the door and stepped out onto the sidewalk in front of the restaurant.

He paused and looked toward the water.

"Dean, what is it?" Maddie grabbed his arm as he started to walk toward the bay. "Where are you going?"

"That's Ricardo over there! I can't believe he came all the way here to harass you!" Dean tried to pull away from her grasp.

Maddie's heart pounded as she recognized Ricardo. The loan shark who Craig had borrowed money from. The loan shark who, when Craig had been arrested, had threatened her in an attempt to get her to repay his loan.

Maddie tightened her grip. "Don't you dare go over there. He's a dangerous man!"

"Which is exactly why I need to tell him to leave you alone." Dean pushed away her hand.

"Dean, I am telling you to let it go. Do not take one more step." Maddie's voice raised and sharpened at the same time.

Dean froze. Even in his twenties, he still recognized that tone of voice.

"We're going to forget about this, and we're going to have a nice visit. That's it. I don't want to hear anything more about it." Maddie tugged at his arm. He'd grown into a tall and strong young man, but she had the force of a mother determined to protect her child flowing through her and managed to make him stumble back a few steps.

"Mom, we should at least go to the police and report that he's here." Dean turned to face her.

"Absolutely not." Maddie's muscles tensed at the thought of having to confess the underhanded activities of her ex-husband over the last few years of their marriage, to Jake. "What could they do, anyway? Unless he actually makes contact with me, we have no reason to be concerned."

"No reason to be concerned?" Dean's blue eyes widened as he looked back at her. "Mom! He wouldn't have come all the way here, if he didn't intend to make you pay for Dad's debts."

"Dean, if he so much as looks in my direction, I'll make sure that the police are notified. All right?" Maddie sighed. "Please, I don't want this to ruin your visit. I don't want to think about what happened with your father, or Ricardo, or any of it. I just want to enjoy my life. Can we just go to the marina and enjoy some time together?"

"Fine, yes." Dean put his hands in his pockets. "You're going to make me get on that boat, aren't you?"

"I'm sure you're going to love it once you're on it." Maddie grinned, then looked over her shoulder in the direction of the restaurant. She found Tammy standing just outside the door. She wondered how much she might have overheard.

# CHAPTER 4

"eady for an adventure?" Maddie called out to Tammy.

"Always!" Tammy walked over to Maddie and Dean. She handed Dean his bag, then tossed an arm around each of their shoulders and steered them in the direction of the marina. "I settled things up inside."

"Thank you." Maddie kissed her cheek.

"Thanks, Aunt Tammy."

"You're welcome." Tammy smiled. "I can't believe how much the marina has already changed. When we were kids, it was such a dump, but a great place to play hide-and-seek, right?"

"Right." Maddie recalled the games they played.

"You were always the best at hiding, and you always got me into so much trouble!"

"Trouble?" Dean smiled.

"It wasn't my fault." Tammy pouted as she paused beside Sam's boat.

"She would fall asleep every time." Maddie groaned. "It would take forever for me to find her, and a few times I even had to go home and admit to our parents that I'd lost her. Then Daddy would scour the marina until he found her."

"He always did find me." Tammy's voice grew wistful.

"Welcome aboard!" Sam stood at the top of the ramp that led to the boat. "You three look ready for a real seafaring adventure!"

"Absolutely." Tammy headed up the ramp, with Maddie following behind her.

Maddie coasted her hand along the thin, metal chain that served as a railing for the ramp. She felt a bolt of excitement just to be out on the bay again. It had been many years since she'd gone for a real boat ride across the water.

"How long is the tour?" Dean made his way up the ramp last.

"Just about forty-five minutes. It depends on what we discover out there." Sam gestured to a bench with cushions near the back of the boat. "It's just the three of you on this tour, so make yourselves comfortable, and we'll head out in just a few minutes."

"Thanks, Captain Niles." Maddie searched his face for any hint of familiarity. "You're not from around here, are you?"

"I just set up shop in the marina a little while ago." Sam returned the scrutiny. "Are you a local?"

"I used to be." Maddie smiled. "I guess I am again now."

"Well then, welcome home, lass." Sam winked at her, then walked off toward the front of the boat.

"Wow, I can see why you would want to live here." Dean leaned against the railing at the back of the boat.

"It is beautiful, isn't it?" Tammy smiled as she sat down on the bench.

Maddie sat down beside her and leaned into her shoulder.

"Especially with the two of you here."

"I can see things are really getting built up." Dean scanned the marina as the boat pulled away from it. "I bet in a few years, it will be unrecognizable."

"I'm not so sure that's a good thing." Tammy

winced. "The small shops and houses are being overtaken by the new builds."

"I'm sure it has its pros and cons." Maddie stared at the same buildings. "The property values are certainly going up."

Moments later, a crackling over the PA system drew their attention.

"Captain Niles here. We're setting off on our journey. Have your cameras ready to capture the wonders I point out along the way."

Maddie settled back and gazed out across the open water. She felt herself relax in a way that she hadn't experienced in some time, as ripples carried across the expanse. She glanced over at Tammy and recognized the wistful expression that softened her features.

"It's so beautiful here." Tammy brushed her blonde hair back behind her ears as a breeze whipped off the water.

As Sam rattled on over the PA system, Maddie's focus remained on the familiar sights around her. No matter how someone else described them, they would always be defined by her memories from the past.

"Do you remember when we were stranded in

the middle of the harbor?" The long-forgotten memory bolted to the surface. "It was so dark!"

"Absolutely, I remember!" Tammy leaned closer to her. "It was all your fault!"

"It wasn't." Maddie gasped. "It was yours. If you hadn't followed me, I never would have lost the paddle."

"I followed you because you snuck out! You weren't supposed to be anywhere near the bay." Tammy rolled her eyes. "But of course, you had to do what you pleased. You couldn't possibly be expected to follow the rules."

"That didn't mean that you had to follow me." Maddie frowned, then laughed as she shook her head. "This is just like the argument we had that night. I still remember you taking that flying leap off the dock. I thought you had lost your mind."

"I thought you would leave me there in the water." Tammy's voice softened. "But you didn't."

"Of course not. I pulled you in." Maddie grinned as she leaned back against the cushions on the bench. "But when I pulled you in, one of the paddles fell out." She nudged Dean with her elbow. "You should have seen me trying to paddle our way back to the dock with one paddle. It didn't go well."

"I can picture it." Dean laughed, then looked

between the two of them. "So, how did you get back? Did you swim?"

"No, we were too far out for that." Maddie looked over the water. "It was too dark to see us on the water, and no one knew that we were out there. But magically, a rescue boat happened to be patrolling, and towed us back to the dock. Remember, Tammy? I'll always be grateful for whatever force or magic made that boat go out on patrol."

"Oh, it wasn't a force or magic. It was Jake." Tammy smiled as the boat turned back toward the marina.

"What do you mean it was Jake?" Maddie gripped the cushion on the seat as the boat rocked slightly during its turn.

"He's the one who called out the boat patrol. He's the reason we didn't end up floating out to sea. Didn't you know that?" Tammy looked over at her.

"No, I had no idea." The memory of the rescue boat arriving to save them, took on a different feeling. "How did he even know we were out there?"

"Honestly, I never asked." Tammy shrugged. "He must have seen us from the dock, I guess."

"But it was so dark." Maddie pursed her lips as

she ran through every detail she could recall of that night.

"Does it matter?" Tammy nudged Maddie's knee with her own. "The important thing is that we're still around to tell the tale."

"True." Maddie sat forward as the dock came into view. She noticed a gathering of people waiting for the next tour. "Did you like the ride, Dean?" She glanced over at her son.

"It was nice." Dean offered her his hand to help her to her feet. "I guess if you have to live so far away, I'm glad it's here."

"Don't you worry, Dean." Maddie stood up as the boat rocked and steadied him when he stumbled. "I may be far away, but I'll never be too far to look out for you."

"I see that." Dean laughed as he regained his balance.

As they disembarked, Sam greeted the next group of passengers.

"Welcome aboard!"

"Sam Niles, I need a word!" a man in the back of the crowd shouted.

"Not now, I'm busy." Sam's accent and joviality vanished.

"You can give me five minutes now, or I can

make sure this boat doesn't leave the dock."

The sharpness of the man's tone drew Maddie's attention to him. His height surprised her, as he towered above the others gathered near the boat. His broad shoulders and thick chest indicated a muscular frame. His bushy, brown eyebrows furrowed and added a shadow to his already dark expression.

"Let's move along." Maddie shooed Dean and Tammy ahead of her. She didn't want to get involved. She just wanted to enjoy their time together. As she walked away from the boat, she noticed Lawson, the man who had been having coffee with Tim at Janet's, in the queue waiting to board the boat. He had obviously taken Tim's advice and decided to enjoy the scenery.

As they headed back in the direction of the house, Maddie glanced over her shoulder in time to see Sam step down onto the dock and move away from the crowd with the man who demanded his attention. She noticed Lawson follow Sam over to the man.

"What do you think that was about?" Tammy shielded her eyes as she looked in the direction of the dock.

"I'm not sure, but nothing we need to be in the

middle of, I'm certain." Maddie forced confidence into her tone, but her mind had already begun doing cartwheels of curiosity. Who was the man? Why did he think he could intimidate Sam into getting his attention?

The moment Maddie set foot on the front porch, a volley of barks sounded from beyond the front door.

"Girls!" Dean cried out as he reached for the door. "I've missed you so much!"

Maddie opened the door, and Bella and Polly bounded forward to greet Dean. He fell to his knees to pat them as they ran in circles around him. They tried to get as close as possible for his affection.

"Oh, now I see who you really came here to visit." Maddie grinned. "I'm here, too, you know!" She reached down to pet the dogs.

"These two are seriously the sweetest pups in the world." Dean ruffled their white fur, then ushered them inside.

Maddie's heart warmed at the sight of Dean and the dogs. A quick ache filled her at the thought of him leaving. Her mind traveled back to the first day she'd sent him off to school. How had so many years passed, and yet the same feeling could flow through her as if not a single second had gone by?

# CHAPTER 5

fter getting Dean settled in his room, and showing him around the house, Maddie headed to the kitchen to make a fresh pot of coffee.

When it was ready, she poured them all a cup as Tammy joined her in the kitchen.

"Thank you." Tammy took the cup and followed Maddie into the dining room. "Now, it's time to get to work."

Tammy spent the rest of the afternoon pulling wallpaper off the walls with Dean, as Maddie worked in the room upstairs she had set up as an office. The view across the bay from the small room was spectacular, and she often caught herself staring out across it. The dogs happily had a nap in the dog bed they shared in the office. Although Maddie had bought them individual beds, they always shared one, cuddled close together.

Maddie had a few bookkeeping clients, but it wasn't something she loved to do, and it wasn't enough to pay the bills. She needed to find another job. Hopefully, something she enjoyed, but she couldn't be picky. When Maddie had finished her work, she went downstairs to take the dogs outside to play for a bit. They happily chased each other around the front yard.

As the afternoon rolled into evening, she walked over to the nearly bare walls.

"Dean, you're not here to work. You're supposed to be taking a break for a few days before your new job starts." Maddie glanced at the grandfather clock in one corner of the dining room. "Why don't you go out tonight and see what the town has to offer? Maybe you can find a way to enjoy yourself."

"I did spot a bar by the harbor, and it might be playing the game tonight." Dean's eyes brightened at the thought. "Are you sure you wouldn't mind?"

"Not at all. Go on and have some fun. I'll save some dinner for you, for when you get home." Maddie patted his shoulder.

"Speaking of food." Tammy followed Maddie

into the kitchen as Dean went upstairs. "I invited Amber over tonight. We have an idea, and we wanted to talk to you about it."

Maddie smiled at the thought of her best childhood friend, Amber West, having dinner together with them. She couldn't remember the last time all three of them shared a meal.

"You're teaming up against me?" Maddie placed a few chicken breasts on a pan. "About what?"

"You'll see when she gets here." Tammy glanced at her watch. "She should be here any minute."

"I can't wait to see what you two have cooked up." Maddie began seasoning the chicken. "I'm sure it's something fantastic."

"I think it is." Tammy clasped her hands together and looked into her eyes. "I hope you'll feel the same way."

"Just tell me, Tammy!" Maddie laughed.

"Not yet, not until Amber gets here."

"Bye, Mom!" Dean called out to her just before the front door opened and closed.

"Bye!" Maddie called back, though the door had already shut. "Love you!" She slid the chicken into the oven.

"Doesn't that bring back memories?" Tammy

grinned. "Supporting you through the teenage years was a very special experience."

"I'm so glad you were on the other end of the line to remind me that we were teenagers once, too." Maddie grabbed a bottle of white wine. "We need to celebrate, since we haven't had dinner together in so long. What are you two cooking up?"

"I'll get the glasses." Tammy rustled through the cabinets as a knock sounded on the front door.

"That must be Amber. I'll let her in." Maddie crossed through the dining room, and the living room, to reach the front hallway. She pulled open the door and smiled at the sight of her friend on the other side.

"Did she tell you yet?" Amber rushed past her, into the house.

"No, not yet. What are you two up to?" Maddie followed her into the kitchen just as Tammy began filling the wineglasses.

"This is from Peter." Amber placed a loaf of sourdough bread on the counter. Peter Wilcox used to work at the bakery when he was a teen. He was a few years older than Maddie, and she had a crush on him when they were growing up. He was now a carpenter but still made the most delicious bread as a hobby.

"Thank you. How is Peter?" Maddie winked at Amber. Amber and Peter had recently started dating.

"Never mind that. Is Dean here?" Amber glanced around. "I can't wait to see him."

"Oh, he's gone out exploring for the evening." Maddie smiled as she accepted one of the glasses from Tammy. "He doesn't want to hang out with his old mother all the time."

"What he doesn't know about how we used to party, he doesn't ever have to know." Tammy grinned as she handed Amber a glass as well.

"Oh, those were the days." Amber clinked her glass against Maddie's. "But what would you know about it, Tammy? You were too young to hang out with us!"

"Are you kidding? I tagged along more times than I can count, but you two were too busy to notice." Tammy clinked her glass against Amber's. "It was fun, though."

"And so long ago." Maddie ran her fingertip along the rim of her glass. "Sometimes it feels like I've lived so many lifetimes, but at other times, it feels like it all went by in the blink of an eye."

"It's wild how much our lives have changed. And yet, here we are." Amber looked into

Maddie's eyes, then Tammy's. "Back where we all started."

"I never thought I'd see the day that I'd move back here." Maddie sat down on the couch.

"Me, neither." Amber sat down beside her. "I love this place. I grew up here, had all of my best memories here. I've never lived anywhere else, and it's kind of nice to have solid foundations here."

"Oh, but you see, Maddie has always been too glamorous for this town." Tammy sat down on the other side of her. "I remember all the plans she made. She wanted to live in the biggest city she could, in the tallest tower she could find. Remember, Maddie? You would draw pictures of it."

"Oh yes, and at one point I did live pretty high up in a building in New York City, another lifetime ago." Maddie took a sip of her wine. "But I gave all that up when Craig wanted to start a family, shortly after we finished college. He convinced me that kids needed a yard to play in, and suddenly my entire life changed again. I had to give up my career, before it even started, and be a mother." She glanced over at Amber. "You've made a wonderful life here. I just never thought I'd be back here."

"I watched you create and raise that family. I saw the beauty of it, and I know what an amazing job you did." Tammy patted Maddie's knee. "Just because Craig turned out to be a terrible person, that doesn't mean that the family you created is any less wonderful."

"I know." Maddie smiled. "Enough talk about that. Now, it's time for the two of you to spill!"

# CHAPTER 6

"Just hear us out!" Amber set her glass of wine down on the coffee table and turned to look at Maddie.

"Don't say no right off the bat." Tammy fixed a stern look on Maddie. "Keep an open mind."

"Out with it!" Maddie groaned. "I can't take the suspense anymore!"

"You should open the bakery." Tammy met her eyes.

"What?" Maddie scrunched up her nose.

"You should open the bakery," Tammy repeated.

"I don't know, Tammy." Maddie glanced away from her sister. "I don't know how to run a bakery, and I don't have any funds to start anything up."

"You grew up in the bakery. I'm sure you picked

up more than you realized, along the way." Tammy clasped her hands together. "We own the bakery, and I can help with the finances."

"You won't need much." Amber pulled a folded-up piece of paper out of her purse. "I have a connection with the board that's offering grants for new businesses opening in the area. All you have to do is fill out this form, and I'm sure that you'll be approved."

"You said you had to find work, right?" Tammy smiled. "Why not just work for yourself? Doesn't it sound exciting?"

"It does," Maddie agreed. "But I would have to hire people to do a lot of the work. It just doesn't seem practical."

"You'd make it work. This place is in dire need of a bakery, and you should open one up before one of those chain places swoops in and does it first." Tammy grabbed Maddie's hand. "What do you think? Will you try it? If not, I think we should sell the place."

"Sell it?" Amber gasped.

"Yes, I don't want the building to just sit empty." Tammy's shoulders slumped. "And you can get the money from the sale to help you out, Maddie."

"I think that's much more practical." Maddie took a sip of her wine.

"Oh, what a shame." Amber tucked the paper back in her purse. "But I understand. If that's really what you want, I can help you out with a Realtor."

"Thanks, Amber." Tammy had a long sip of wine. Maddie detected the disappointment in her sister's voice.

By the time Amber left for the night, and Tammy headed to her room, Maddie was tired. She crawled into bed with Bella and Polly and closed her eyes. The moment she did, her mind began racing. Were they really going to sell the bakery? Was Ricardo still lurking around, waiting for the right time to threaten her?

When she turned over for the third time, Polly whimpered.

"I know, I know, I'm keeping you awake." Maddie stroked her fingers through the warm, soft fur near Polly's cheek. "Why don't we go for a quick walk? Maybe that will help clear my head."

Maddie climbed out of bed, and the dogs followed her every move. As she pulled on some pants and tossed a jacket over her nightgown, she recalled the many late-night walks she would take as a teenager. She thought her mother never knew.

With quiet steps, she crept toward the front door, just as she had so many years ago.

The dogs clambered around her legs, excited to go for a walk.

"Shh." Maddie clipped their leashes on and hurried them out the door.

She'd found out the truth about what her mother knew, during a visit to her parents' house when she was in her thirties. Craig was reading a book. Her kids were tucked in their beds, sound asleep, but she couldn't rest. She'd started her routine of sneaking out the door, only to find her mother waiting for her, already bundled in her jacket, with a flashlight in her hand. On that walk, they had shared so much with one another, about being wives, and mothers, and what the future might hold.

Maddie flicked on her flashlight and closed the door carefully behind her. Her heart ached with a sudden longing for her mother, for her company, for her laughter, for her no-nonsense looks that put her in her place, no matter how old she was.

As Maddie walked, her mind began to wonder as she let the dogs lead the way. They kept their noses to the ground as they found their way to the beach.

"I thought I left all of the chaos behind." Her

heart raced at the memory of seeing Ricardo. How long would it take him to find her? What would she do when he confronted her? She'd told him before that he needed to collect what he felt he was owed from Craig, not her. But he didn't care about their divorce. He didn't care that Craig was behind bars. He'd insisted that he held her just as responsible for the debt her ex-husband owed. She shivered as she recalled the twisted smile that Ricardo gave her when she pleaded with him to be reasonable. Criminals like that weren't reasonable.

The dogs tugged her forward, eager to get to the edge of the water, but she steered them back away from it. Bringing home a couple of wet dogs wouldn't make it any easier to sleep.

Instead, she guided them down the beach in the direction of the harbor. Soon, the other end of the harbor would have an amusement park that would bring all kinds of visitors to the town. Soon, the dilapidated buildings that intermingled with brand new structures would completely vanish, and the town would never again be as she remembered it.

"Good." Maddie smiled to herself at the thought. "That's exactly what this place needs, a fresh start, just like me." Her thoughts were interrupted when the dogs began barking and growling as they approached the area where they were building a new pier. It was separated by a chain-link fence.

"What is it, girls? Calm down!" Maddie tightened her grip on their leashes. "You're going to wake the whole town!"

The dogs lunged toward the fence and continued to bark.

The sudden movement surprised Maddie, and she stumbled a few steps. As she tried to catch her balance, her foot caught on a brick near the fence. She slammed into the fence and managed to catch herself on it without falling.

A sharp breath rushed into her lungs as the dogs continued to bark. The dogs' incessant barks made her heart race. She tugged them away from the fence and back in the direction of home. She instinctively reached for her phone in case she needed to call for help, but it wasn't there. She realized she must have left it at home.

An icy sensation carried through her as she guided the dogs toward home. Something was wrong!

# CHAPTER 7

"Shh, girls, please. We're going to go home. Everything's okay," Maddie murmured to them as she quickened her pace.

She ran down the paths that were familiar to her in many ways and managed to make it back to her house in record time.

As Maddie reached her house, she heard sirens and saw red and blue lights splashed across her fence as the police cars sped past in the direction of the harbor.

A rush of panic flooded through her. Something had happened, but what?

Maddie quickly walked toward her front door. Her hand trembled as she attempted to slide her key into the lock. She tried to slow down her breathing and get her heartbeat under control. Why was she so flustered?

The knob turned before she could get the key into the lock. The door swung open.

"Maddie?" Tammy stared out at her with wide eyes and a half-open mouth. "I thought you were a burglar, until I saw you through the window."

"Not a burglar." The dogs rushed past Tammy, into the house, and tugged Maddie along with them. "Sorry for waking you."

"Where were you?" Tammy glanced at a clock on the wall. "It's almost eleven!"

"I know. I just needed to go for a walk to clear my head." Maddie shivered at the memory of the sensation she felt when she was by the harbor. As if someone was watching her.

"Maddie? What's wrong?" Tammy stared at her as she released the dogs from their leashes. "You look so pale!"

"I'm fine, just tired." Maddie shrugged off her jacket. "I think something happened down at the harbor. I saw the police headed that way."

"Oh, I wonder what happened?"

"I'm sure we'll find out tomorrow. I just want to get some sleep. I'm sorry for waking you, Tammy." Maddie followed the dogs up the stairs toward her bedroom and closed the door behind her.

The dogs pawed at her legs, eager to cuddle up in bed.

Maddie lifted them up onto the bed. As she sprawled across the mattress, the dogs curled up on either side of her. What had they sensed at the harbor? What had happened? They didn't seem to dwell on it. Instead, they easily fell asleep.

Maddie stared at the ceiling as her thoughts wandered from the dogs' barking to the police lights, then to Ricardo. She tried to relax as she rested her head on her pillow. Despite her racing heart, she soon fell asleep.

It felt as if she'd only closed her eyes for a moment, when knocking on the front door riled the dogs. They ran to the bedroom door and barked. Polly scratched at the corner of it in an attempt to open it.

"Okay, settle down, girls, settle down. It's just someone at the door."

Still groggy, the night before began to unfold in her mind as she threw a robe over her nightgown and the pants she'd worn the night before. Through her bedroom door, she heard muffled voices.

Tammy, and who else?

Maddie's eyes flew wide open as she recognized the full, heavy tone of his voice. Why was he there?

Maybe, if the dogs hadn't been barking so loudly, she could pretend to be asleep, and he would leave. But no one could sleep through that noise. She glanced in the mirror at her disheveled hair, frizzy around her pale face. Tiredness darkened the bright shade of her blue eyes.

"Get yourself together, Maddie." She glared at her reflection. A quick pinch to each of her cheeks provided some color, and a wide smile managed to force some light into her gaze.

She opened the bedroom door.

Bella and Polly ran straight down the stairs toward the front door, where Jake stood, with his hat in his hands. He dropped his gaze to them, then lifted it sharply in Maddie's direction.

"Maddie, Jake's come to visit." Tammy smiled as she looked over at her. "I'm sorry, I know you didn't get much sleep last night."

"You didn't?" Jake crouched down, though his gaze remained on Maddie. He held out his hands to Bella and Polly.

The two dogs stopped barking and licked his outstretched fingers instead.

"Oh, this old place, with its creaks and knocks." Maddie paused a few feet away from him.

"Would you like some coffee, Jake?" Tammy gestured to the kitchen.

"Thanks, I could use a cup." Jake stood back up to his full height. "I was out late last night as well."

Maddie wondered if he'd grown a full foot since she knew him in high school. His shoulders spread wider than she ever recalled. Her throat grew dry as she prepared herself for his next questions. Why was he there?

Jake's green eyes probed hers, stern and curious. "I'm investigating a crime."

"A crime?" Tammy gasped from the kitchen. "What crime?" She stuck her head out through the door. "Who did it?"

"That's what I'm trying to find out." Jake smiled as he accepted the cup of coffee she offered. "I thought maybe Maddie would be able to help me with that."

"Maddie?" Tammy scrunched up her nose as she handed Maddie her cup. "Why? She's not a psychic, you know?"

"Tammy, would you mind if I spoke with Maddie alone for a moment?" Jake's tone remained polite, with a hint of strain.

"I guess that's up to Maddie." Tammy crossed her arms over the silky, vibrant-colored dress she wore. "Maddie?"

Jake cleared his throat as he tried to meet Maddie's eyes.

Maddie nodded to Tammy.

"It's fine. Whatever you need, Jake, of course." She paused, then met his gaze. "Or should I say Chief? Is this an official visit?"

"It is." Jake's smile vanished. "But Jake is fine."

"So, what is this about?" Maddie's heartbeat quickened at the seriousness of his gaze.

"Last night, someone called and reported dogs barking loudly. The person who called thought they might be loose. When one of my officers went out to the harbor, the dogs were gone. But he found a man. Dead!" Jake paused as he watched her reaction. "Murdered!"

# CHAPTER 8

"*M*urdered?" Maddie gasped.

"Maddie, was it you out there with your dogs?" Jake shifted closer to her, his voice hard, but quiet.

"Yes." Maddie's heart raced. "But I had no idea that someone had been murdered."

"What were you doing out there so late? Alone?" Jake's brows knitted together as he looked into her eyes. "Or was Dean with you?"

"No. It was just me." Maddie felt Bella pawing at her leg, and knew the dog sensed her shock. "I had a hard time sleeping, so I took the girls out for a walk."

"Why were the dogs barking?" Jake's forehead

relaxed as he reached down to stroke the top of Bella's head. "Were they upset about something?"

"I'm so sorry about all of the noise. Will I need to pay a fine or something?" Maddie tried to shoo Bella away, but the dog insisted on licking Jake's fingers.

"No, not at all. But I do need to ask you a few questions." Jake gestured to the dining room table. "Could we sit for a few minutes?"

"Of course. Sorry about the mess." Maddie sat down at the table.

"Maddie." Jake sat down opposite her and pulled out his phone. "Are you familiar with this man?" He held up the phone which displayed a photograph. Maddie's eyes flew wide open as the picture of the man sent her heart racing.

"Ricardo!" Maddie blurted out his name, then cringed.

How would she explain who Ricardo was, and why he'd been in town looking for her? Would Jake find out about the connection? Would he discover the real reason she had moved back home? Of course he would. She could only imagine the rumors that would fly around town. She had already lost her possessions, her money, her marriage, but now she faced the likelihood of losing her good reputation. She knew there was no getting away from it. The truth was going to come out.

"Yes, I'm familiar with him. Was he murdered?"

"Yes, I'm afraid so." Jake cleared his throat. "He was a pretty seedy guy. How were you caught up with him?"

"I'm not caught up with him." Maddie looked down at her folded hands on the table.

"Obviously, not anymore. No one is." Jake leaned forward. "Did you see him last night, Maddie?"

"What?" Maddie gasped. "No, I never saw him."

"It's okay, Maddie, you can talk to me."

Maddie hardened her voice and looked straight at him. "Are you accusing me of something?"

"We found your fingerprints on the fence by the pier they are building." Jake stared back at her. "I know you were there. Why don't you tell me what you saw?"

"Is that where he was killed?" Maddie's heart raced.

"Yes, he was found by the pier."

"Wow." Maddie sat back against the chair.

"Talk to me." Jake sat back in his chair as well. "We're friends, aren't we?"

"Are we?" Maddie heard the sharpness in her

own tone. "I haven't known you for years, Jake, and now you're sitting at my table, asking me if I'm a murderer?"

"I'm not asking you that." Jake gritted his teeth. "I know that you're not."

Stunned by his words, she could only stare at him. She had assumed he suspected her, that he came there to try to trick her into admitting to a crime she didn't commit. When she looked into his eyes, she didn't see deceit. But then, she hadn't known when Craig was lying to her, either.

"You can't know that." Maddie winced as she realized arguing that she could be a murderer, might not be the best direction to go in.

"I do." Jake cleared his throat. "All I want to know is what you saw. From what we can tell from his smart watch, he was dead for a while before the dogs started barking, about forty minutes. Why were they barking?"

"I guess because they sensed Ricardo there." Maddie began to replay the moments in her mind. "We were just out walking, and then they started barking, and lunging toward the fence. I tripped and fell into the fence. They had me on edge with their barking, so I came back home. I didn't see Ricardo. I didn't know what had happened."

"So, you decided to run?" A gruffness entered Jake's voice.

"I didn't run." Maddie avoided his gaze. "I just didn't stay. I could sense someone might be there, and I didn't want to stay there."

"Or you had a good reason not to." Jake picked up his phone and flipped to another picture. When he set it down again between them, his voice and expression grew stern. "That's your husband with Ricardo, isn't it? Craig?"

"Ex-husband." Maddie's heart began to pound as she stared at the picture.

"Was Ricardo here for you? Did he threaten you?" Jake raised an eyebrow. "What contact have you had with Ricardo since he arrived in town?"

"None." Maddie looked at the picture.

"Maddie, I already know that Ricardo arrived in town early yesterday morning. Are you saying he didn't contact you at all?" Jake rapped his knuckles against the table.

"I didn't speak with him. But I did see him. Outside of Janet's Place. By the water." Maddie's heartbeat quickened as she recalled stopping her son from talking to Ricardo. "I don't think he saw me."

"That's when you should have come to me."

Jake slid the phone back into his pocket. "I would have helped you, Maddie."

"I just didn't want to think about it. I just wanted to enjoy my son's visit, and believe that I could live life, without the past coming back to haunt me. And, I guess." Maddie took a breath as she met his eyes. "I didn't want everyone to know my business."

"Where is Dean, now?" Jake glanced toward the hallway that led to the bedrooms. "I need to speak with him."

"I'm sure he's sleeping." Maddie's heart raced at the thought of Dean being questioned by the police. "But he didn't have anything to do with this, Jake, you have to believe me. He's just here to visit me. That's it."

"Go and wake him, please." Jake pointed toward the stairs. "I need to speak with him."

Maddie stood up from her chair.

"Maddie!" Tammy hissed from the doorway of the kitchen.

Maddie looked toward her and caught Jake looking in the same direction. "What is it, Tammy?"

"Dean's not in his room," Tammy spoke in a whisper.

"What did you say?" Jake took a few steps closer to her.

"What?" Maddie kept her eyes on Tammy. "Did he leave early this morning?"

Tammy bit into her bottom lip and looked between the two of them. She grabbed Maddie's arm and pulled her close enough to whisper in her ear, "I don't think he came home last night."

"What was that?" Jake crossed the short distance between them. "You need to tell me where he is."

Maddie didn't know what to say. Where was Dean?

# CHAPTER 9

"*W*here is Dean, Maddie?" Jake's tone sharpened.

"He's not here." Maddie turned toward him. "I don't know where he is. But when I find him, I'll let him know that you need to speak with him."

"Maddie." Jake's jaw rippled with tension. "It's very important that I speak with him. Keeping things from me is not the way to go. Do you understand? I need you to be honest with me."

"As soon as I find him, I'll let you know." Maddie took a step back from him and glanced briefly at Tammy before looking back at Jake. "But like I said, he had nothing to do with any of this. You're better off spending your time looking for the murderer, not barking up the wrong tree."

"I'm going to try to find him, but if I can't, I'm going to trust you, Maddie." Jake held her gaze as his voice softened. "I'm going to trust you to bring Dean to me for a conversation. Don't let him skip town. Okay?"

"Okay," Maddie replied as Bella and Polly wound around her legs, eager to get her attention.

Jake nodded to her, then to Tammy, before starting toward the door.

Maddie held her breath. She expected him to turn around and demand information, or even threaten to arrest her. Instead, he closed the door quietly behind him.

"Maddie, what is going on? Do you think Dean killed Ricardo? I mean, I wouldn't blame him. If I had the chance, I would have killed him myself."

"Tammy! Don't talk like that. Jake could be listening. He could be right outside the door, or he could have planted a bug!" Maddie peered at the front door.

"A bug? Don't you think you're being a little paranoid?" Tammy looked toward the door as well.

"Tammy, you know I love you, and how positive you always are, but this is a murder investigation. Do you get that?" Maddie pressed her hand against her chest. "If Dean is convicted, he could face life in prison."

"We won't let that happen!" Tammy grabbed Maddie's shoulders and looked into her eyes. "We'll find out the truth. Dean will be fine."

"Thank you, Tammy." Maddie felt grateful that her sister was there. Craig had always been her partner while raising the kids, but now she felt as if she had no one to turn to. Tammy proved otherwise.

The front door swung open, and Dean stepped inside.

Bella and Polly raced toward him. He crouched down to pat their heads.

"We'll play more later, girls. I need a nap." Dean stood up and headed for the stairs that led to the bedrooms.

"Dean!" Maddie's heart lurched with a mixture of relief and panic as she followed him. "Dean, where were you?"

"I just need some sleep, Mom. I'm so tired." Dean continued toward the stairs.

Maddie caught him by his arm and guided him away from the hallway, toward the living room.

"Mom! What are you doing?" Dean's voice raised.

"I need to talk to you." Maddie pointed to the couch. Bella and Polly followed after them.

"What's going on?" Dean looked over at Tammy for an explanation as he sat down on the couch. Polly jumped into his lap, and Bella nestled beside him. "What is this about?"

Tammy held up her hands and winced.

"It's about Ricardo." Maddie drew his attention back to her. "What did you do, Dean? Did you go looking for him? Where were you?"

"Mom!" Dean held out his hands as he looked up at her. "What do you want me to say? Yes, I went looking for him, and yes, I told him to leave you alone. How could I not? Do you think I'm just going to stand aside and let him harass you?"

"Dean, what did you do?" Maddie's voice wavered.

"Mom, what's wrong?" Dean rubbed his hand along Bella's back. "I just spoke to him. That's all."

"Ricardo was found dead last night." Tammy sat down on the couch on the other side of Dean and draped her arm around his shoulders.

"What?" Dean gasped. The dogs looked up at him, then laid their heads down again.

"Apparently, your mom was near the crime scene when she was out walking the dogs late last night, just before he was found. It's been quite a shock, and now the police are looking for you."

"For me?" Dean's voice trailed off as his eyes widened. "Do they think I killed him?"

"I don't know what they think." Maddie clasped her hands together. "But we need to get your story straight before you speak to them."

"My story?" Dean stared into her eyes. "I didn't do this! You know that, don't you? I just spoke to him! I didn't touch him!"

"Of course you didn't." Maddie hugged him. Polly leaned up to lick her cheek as she pulled away.

"You didn't think I would do something like that, did you?" Dean's jaw tensed. "I would never kill anyone."

"Of course I didn't think you did." Maddie took a step back. "But I needed you to tell me everything. Now, we have to figure this out."

"Figure what out?" Dean asked incredulously. "I'm innocent, Mom. I'll just tell the police that."

"That's not always how these things work. Sometimes being innocent isn't enough. Where were you all night? Why didn't you come home?" Maddie sat on the couch beside him with Bella nestled between them.

"I was out." Dean cleared his throat.

"Now isn't the time to be bashful." Tammy patted his arm. "Were you with someone? You can tell us."

"I have a girlfriend. I would never do that. I was alone. I had a couple of drinks at the bar. I wanted to find out why Ricardo was here, and how much Dad owed him. I thought maybe I could pay Ricardo off, so that he would leave you alone." Dean looked up at his mother. "But of course, I couldn't just ask Dad."

"Is that when you went looking for him?" Maddie searched his eyes. "For Ricardo?"

"Yes. I thought since I couldn't get hold of Dad to tell me, Ricardo would. When I found him, I wanted to know how much Dad owed, and I offered to pay it off, so he would leave you alone. But he blew me off, like he didn't have time for me. He said it wasn't important, and he took off." Dean cleared his throat. "He was messing with my head. I figured he planned to ask for double, so he was stringing me along."

"What then?" Tammy leaned closer to him. "Did you go after him?"

"No. I was worried that I had made things worse. That's why I didn't come home. I didn't want to lead him right to your door. I stayed on one of the bus benches near the marina." Dean sighed. "I'm sorry, Mom. I guess I did make a mess of things."

"You were only trying to protect me. I understand that. But one of these days, you're going to have to accept the fact that I don't need anyone's protection." Maddie patted his knee. "Now, we just have to make sure that this situation doesn't get worse."

"How are we going to do that?" Dean's cheeks flushed. "Maybe I should just get out of town while I can. If I'm not around, then the police can't do anything to me, right?"

"No." Maddie squeezed his hand. "I can't let you do that. It will only make you look guilty if you take off. We have to face this, head-on."

"What do you mean?" Dean looked into her eyes. "How?"

"I'm going to take you down to the police station." Maddie stood up from the couch. "You're going to give your statement."

"My statement?" Dean stared up at her. "Mom. I can't do that. If I tell them that I had an argument with Ricardo, they'll arrest me right then and there."

"So, don't tell them." Tammy looked over at him. "You don't have to share everything."

"I don't know about that." Maddie looked

between the two of them. "If you don't tell the truth, it could come back to hurt you later."

"Aunt Tammy is right, Mom. I don't have to tell them everything. I didn't kill Ricardo, so it doesn't matter. I'll just answer their questions. Nothing more. That way it looks like I'm cooperating." Dean stood up from the couch and the dogs jumped down. "Maybe it will be enough for them to leave me alone."

"You shouldn't hide things from them. You don't have an alibi for the time that Ricardo was killed. Unfortunately, I think you're going to remain on the suspect list. The sooner you go into the station and give your statement, the less suspicious the police will be." Maddie walked over to the table by the front door and picked up her purse. "Let's go now, Dean."

Dean hesitated as he lingered beside the couch. "I should at least change and wash up first."

"All right." Maddie studied the clothing he wore. A part of her wondered if they should destroy it. A pang of guilt silenced the idea. Did she really suspect him? Of course not. Now she had to do everything in her power to help prove he was innocent, by finding the real murderer.

# CHAPTER 10

"*M*addie, what can I do?" Tammy joined her by the door.

"There's nothing you can do." Maddie placed her hand on her arm. "There's no point in putting it off. Jake will find Dean soon enough and demand to question him. At least if we go in willingly, he might see that as a good sign."

"I'm sure he will." Tammy grabbed her purse. "I'll come with you."

"No. You stay here with the dogs. I don't know what's going to happen. I might need to get him a lawyer."

"A friend of Brad's is a criminal lawyer. I can reach out to him, and see if he has any advice."

Tammy pulled her phone out of her pocket to call her husband.

"Great, thank you, Tammy." Maddie took a deep breath.

"I'll call him right away!" Tammy turned toward the hallway as Dean stepped out into it. "Stay strong, Dean. You're going to be just fine."

"Right, Aunt Tammy." Dean scrunched up his nose as he walked toward his mother. "Mom, are you going to the police station in your robe?"

"Oh, dear." Maddie looked down at her robe. "Give me a second to change." She pointed her finger at him. "Don't you even think about leaving this house without me."

"I'll be right here, Mom."

As Maddie hurried to change, she thought about Jake's words. Would he really be her ally? She couldn't risk Dean's freedom by trusting that he would be.

Maddie said goodbye to the dogs. As she stepped into the living room, Dean opened the front door for her.

"Mom, let's get this over with."

Maddie wrapped her arm around his. "It'll be over before you know it."

"Somehow, I don't think that's going to be the case." Dean held the door for her.

"Don't forget, Dean, I grew up here. I still know most of the people in this town. They're going to be on our side."

"I'm not sure that's going to matter." Dean settled in the passenger side of her car. "I just hope that they quickly find out who actually killed Ricardo, so the cops can leave me alone, and I can buy him a steak dinner."

"That's exactly the kind of talk that's going to raise suspicions." Maddie closed her door and shot him a look of warning. "This isn't a joke, Dean. Ricardo might not have been the best person in the world, but no one deserves to be murdered."

"I know." Dean stared out through the windshield. "But should he really have been allowed to go around threatening people? You?" He looked over at her as she started the car. "You never did a single thing to deserve this, Mom."

"That may be so." Maddie pulled out into the road. "But it doesn't change where we're at right at this moment. But it's all going to be sorted out. Just remember to be polite to the police officer that questions you. Be honest, and always think before you speak." She continued to lecture him as she pulled up in front of the police station and stepped out of the car.

"Mom, relax. I've seen enough television to know what to do and not to do." Dean walked up to the front door and held it open for her.

"That's your best source of information, television?" Maddie winced.

"I think we need to check in here." Dean led her toward a large front desk, with a female officer perched behind it.

Maddie stepped forward and tried to get the officer's attention.

"We're here to see Jake." She cleared her throat. "I mean, the chief."

"Oh?" The woman peered at her from behind small, circular glasses that magnified the size of her dark brown eyes. "Do you have an appointment?"

"Just let him know that Maddie and Dean are here. I'm sure that he'll want to see us." Maddie glanced over at Dean and felt a sudden urge to tell him to run. Was it the right choice to walk him into the police station? Would he be walking back out with her?

"It's okay, Noreen, I'm here." Jake looked at the police officer as he walked up to the front desk. He cast a brief smile at Maddie, before focusing his attention on Dean. "Dean, would you come with me?"

"I'm coming along." Maddie adjusted the purse strap on her shoulder as her muscles tensed.

"Mom, it's okay." Dean rubbed her shoulder. "I won't be long."

"Absolutely not, Dean. You're not going anywhere without me."

"Don't worry, Maddie." Jake looked at Dean. "I'll take good care of him."

Protectiveness threatened to make Maddie object, but she resisted. She didn't want to make things any worse for her son.

"It's okay, Mom." Dean gave her a quick hug, then followed Jake down a long hallway lined with identical doors.

Maddie clenched her teeth as she tried to ignore the urge to chase after them.

"I'll get you a coffee, dear." Noreen stepped out from behind the counter and revealed her short stature as she made her way to the coffeepot.

Maddie clutched her purse strap tightly. She wanted to be in the room as Jake questioned her son, but both had made it clear that she wasn't welcome.

"Here you go." Noreen made her way back with

a small, white cup and held it out to her. "There's some cream and sugar over there, if you'd like."

"Thank you." Maddie took the cup of coffee and met the woman's eyes. "My son is just here to help out with the investigation."

"You don't owe me any explanation." Noreen patted her arm. "I've seen plenty of worried mothers in my day. They all sang the same song, about how innocent their child was. Some were right, some were wrong, but they all loved their babies." She shrugged. "We do our best to protect them when they are little, but once they're on their own, there's not much we can do."

"Well, in my case, I know I'm right." Maddie clutched the cup so tight that a bit of the hot liquid spilled over the rim and trickled across her skin.

"I'm sure you are." Noreen winked at her, then walked back to her perch.

Maddie sat down in an empty chair and fixed her gaze on the large clock on the far wall of the reception area. She watched the second hand swirl, circling again and again. The once hot cup of coffee she held became lukewarm, and then cool. She had yet to take a sip, when she heard Dean's voice.

"Of course, I'll let you know if I think of anything else." Dean met his mother's eyes as he neared the doors of the police station. "Ready to go, Mom?"

"I'll be right out." Maddie watched as he pulled open the door and stepped out. She easily read the tension in his muscles. "That took longer than I expected." She settled her gaze on Jake, then began to follow after her son.

"Thanks for bringing him in." Jake walked with her toward the front door. "I appreciate your cooperation."

"I just wanted you to see for yourself that my son had nothing to do with any of this." Maddie stopped a few feet short of the door and turned to look at him. "I'll be organizing a lawyer for him."

"Maddie, it doesn't have to be like that." Jake met her eyes. "I'm going to have more questions for him, for both of you."

"You can contact his lawyer. I need to make sure we are protected." Maddie turned back toward the door and took a step forward.

"Wait a moment, Maddie." Jake's tone remained civil. "Instead of arguing with me, why don't you help me find the real murderer and make sure that your son's name is cleared."

"Isn't that your job?" Maddie tried to process his offer.

"It certainly is." Jake studied her. "But that doesn't mean that I have to do it alone. You are my connection to Ricardo. You are my connection to Dean. You know him better than I could ever know him. If you say he's innocent, I am inclined to believe you. But a mother's word doesn't erase evidence. It doesn't stop the gears of the justice system from turning. Do you want to stand by and hope that his lawyer is good enough to protect him, or do you want to make sure that if your son is innocent, he will never be arrested?" He stared at her. "I am giving you a chance here, Maddie. I told you before, I am trusting you. All you have to do is trust me, and we can make sure that Ricardo's murderer is brought to justice, with no one else getting trampled along the way. What do you say?"

Maddie searched his eyes for any hint of his true intentions. He claimed that he trusted her, but how could he? He hadn't known her in years. It didn't seem customary for the chief of police to pull a suspect into the investigation. But as he stood there, his expression stern and his eyes locked to hers, she didn't sense any bad intentions. Of course, that didn't mean there weren't any. Slowly, she came to a realization.

"All right, Jake." Maddie offered him her hand. "I guess we'll be partners, then?"

"Partners." A sudden smile engulfed Jake's lips as he took her hand and squeezed it. "We'll get it all figured out, Maddie. One step at a time. Get Dean home. I'll text you with any updates or questions I have. I'll be in touch." He released her hand, then turned and walked back toward the nearly empty reception area.

Maddie stepped out onto the sidewalk in front of the police station to find Dean hovering close by.

"What was that all about?" Dean narrowed his eyes. "Did you tell him that I'm going to get a lawyer?"

"I did." Maddie glanced over her shoulder at the police station, then looked back at him. "But he asked for my help, to find the murderer, to clear your name. I agreed to give it."

"What?" Dean sighed as he rolled his eyes toward the sky. "Mom, you know that's a trick!"

"I know." Maddie smiled some as she led him toward her car. "I know that he thinks he's going to prey on my emotions and get all the details he needs to make a conviction. But he doesn't know that I know that." She snapped her fingers. "And we can use that to our advantage. What better way to prepare for the charges he might level against you than to pretend to be his ally."

"Smart." Dean opened the door to the car for her. "Very smart."

"I've learned a lot over the last year." Maddie settled in the driver's seat and stared out through the windshield at the large window of the police station. "When someone asks you to trust them, it's best to be cautious."

"You trust me, though? You believe I didn't kill him, don't you?" Dean buckled his seat belt.

"Of course." Maddie glanced over at him. "Look, I didn't do it. You didn't do it. But someone killed Ricardo, and our best chance of putting all of this behind us, is to find out who did." She started the engine. "So, that is exactly what we're going to do."

## CHAPTER 11

 M addie parked in her driveway and smiled at the sight of Bella and Polly racing toward the front gate.

"Hi, babies!" She opened the gate and stepped into the yard, eager to greet them. Just a few nuzzles and licks immediately made her smile.

"Dean!" Tammy called out from the front porch. "How did it go?"

"No worries, Aunt Tammy. I was careful and cooperative."

"Good, I'm glad to hear that. Listen, I need to steal your mother away for a little while, okay?" Tammy glanced over at Maddie, who tossed a ball for the dogs.

"For what?" Maddie tugged the ball free of Polly's mouth and tossed it again. "I think it would be best if I stay close to Dean."

"I'm just going to get some sleep, Mom. I'm so tired." Dean trudged up the steps and into the house.

"Dean will be fine, I promise." Tammy watched Dean, then looked back at Maddie. "There's something Amber and I want to show you. I'm sure you could use a distraction right now."

"That's the last thing I need. I need to focus on finding out who killed Ricardo."

"What better way to find a murderer than to create a taskforce?" Tammy grinned as she ushered the dogs into the house.

Maddie looked up at the house as it loomed against the midmorning sky. There were so many memories in that house.

"Let's go!" Tammy hummed a tune as she caught her arm and pulled her toward the car.

"Where are we going?"

"Not far. I'll drive." Tammy took the keys from her. "I spoke to Brad's friend. He isn't available to come here for a few days. But he doesn't think Dean has anything to worry about." She slipped into the car and started the engine.

Maddie climbed in beside her.

"Good, that's a relief."

"And of course, it's good that the chief of police is your friend." Tammy backed out of the driveway.

"We're not friends." Maddie stared through the windshield. "We were never friends."

"Not exactly." Tammy glanced over at her. "But you were there for each other whenever needed. Remember the time you broke Paul Chumley's nose? I don't know if he was more shocked or embarrassed."

"Ugh, Chumley." Maddie rolled her eyes. "I'd forgotten all about him. I didn't mean to actually hurt him, but he had it coming."

"He did. But it wasn't until he started picking on Jake that you let him have it. It was awful the way he cornered Jake. He was so scrawny back then. He wouldn't have stood a chance, if you hadn't shown up." Tammy drove down the street with a smile on her lips. "You weren't having any of it."

"Someone had to shut him down." Maddie crossed her arms. "It had nothing to do with it being Jake. I was just tired of his attitude."

"Are you sure about that?" Tammy turned down another street. "You seemed pretty angry."

"You should have seen how angry Jake was at

me after. I tried to help him up, and he told me that violence was never the answer." Maddie pursed her lips. "I stood up for him, saved him from a bully, and he acted like I did something wrong!"

"He was probably just embarrassed. You know how guys can be when a woman does something they can't." Tammy rolled her eyes.

"I don't know. Jake was never like that. He was always such a rule follower. I really believe he would have preferred to take that beating that day. I never thought he would be the chief of police." Maddie's eyes widened at the sight of the bakery. "What's this? It looks amazing!"

"Amber and I have been working on it, so that it wouldn't be too much of a mess when we sell it. Hopefully, we'll get more for it." Tammy parked beside Amber's car. "We've got the outside pretty cleaned up, but the inside is going to take some work." She led the way into the bakery. "I wanted you to see it."

Maddie ran her fingertips along the golden rim of the front counter as she passed by it. The sensation of the smooth, cool surface against her skin sparked memories of doing the same thing every time she entered the bakery. Usually, it would be right after school. She'd look up to see her father at the register.

Now, she looked up at the empty space where he once stood.

"Maddie, are you with me?" Tammy waved her hand in front of her face. "Amber's going to help us brainstorm while we clean. The three of us can figure out what happened to Ricardo. I'm sure of it. Tell us what you know so far."

"Right." Maddie noticed Amber beside her and gave her a quick hug. "All I know is that Ricardo was here, but he didn't actually come and speak to me. According to Jake, he was here for quite some time, but he never even called me. Which doesn't make a lot of sense, does it?"

"What if he wasn't here to see you?" Amber brushed some dust off the surface of the counter, then looked over at Maddie. "Isn't that possible?"

"Why else would he be here?" Maddie pulled one of the wrought-iron chairs down from the table that matched it and set it upright on the floor.

"Amber has a point." Tammy pulled another chair down. "If he was here to see you, why didn't he confront you? Or even try to speak to you?"

"I don't know." Maddie sat down on the chair

she'd just turned over. "But what are the chances that he'd show up here, if it wasn't about me?"

"From what I've heard around town, it isn't the first time he's been out this way." Amber scanned the ceiling, then winced. "Might need to do some touch-ups on the paint."

"Who else would he be here to see?" Maddie stood up and grabbed an old broom from a corner. As her fingers wound around the old, scarred wooden handle, she felt a bolt of familiarity. It couldn't possibly be the same broom. But it sure felt the same. She'd spent almost every afternoon of her childhood sweeping the bakery floor.

"I'm sure there's no shortage of people who are struggling. If he's a loan shark, he probably has a few customers in the area." Amber continued to wipe off the long counter. "Maybe it's even where Craig met him? While you were here for a visit? When your mother was still alive?"

"I never thought about how Craig got involved with him." Maddie stopped sweeping and looked straight at Amber. "You may be right. His gambling started quite a few years before Mom passed on. I had no idea then, of course, but now that I've looked through all of our financial history, I can definitely see when it started."

"So, if he wasn't here to see you, then we need to find out who he was here to see." Amber met Maddie's eyes.

"But how will we find that out?" Maddie looked between them. "It's not like people are just going to raise their hands and say, 'I borrowed money from a loan shark, who was then murdered'."

"Maybe not, but the rumor mill around here churns out plenty of information." Amber pulled out her phone. "I'll make sure my mother gets right on it. She might be able to turn up something."

"That's great." Maddie smiled at the thought of Amber's mother, Iris, helping her out.

"Just don't forget that you have people here to help you," Amber said.

"Yes, you have Iris, Amber, and me." Tammy pointed at herself. "And it seems to me that Jake is pretty determined to protect you."

"Don't you see, Tammy? That's just a ploy. He wants me to trust him, so that I'll confide in him. He wants me to believe that he doesn't suspect me, so that I'll get comfortable with him, and say something I shouldn't." Maddie shook her head. "The only advantage I have is that he doesn't know I'm onto him."

"Are you sure about that, Maddie?" Amber

leaned against the newly polished counter. "Jake is a pretty honest guy. He's only going to arrest someone, if they're guilty, and I don't think he would try to trick you."

"I hope you're right, but all I know for sure is his goal is to solve this murder." Maddie swept her gaze around her surroundings. Each fixture she looked at came alive with the memory of how glorious it once was. "You were right. We have a lot of work to do in here to get it ready for the sale. But it's going to be great once we're done." She dusted off her hands, then walked toward the door. "I'm going to go talk to Janet. Hopefully, she can help me separate some of the rumors from the truth."

"Keep me up to date on anything you find out." Tammy picked up the broom from the wall where Maddie left it.

"I will." As Maddie stepped out into the sunlight, a flash of a memory of sitting on the curb and sucking on a popsicle, stopped her in her tracks. For just an instant, she saw the bright sun, and the quickly melting popsicle in her hand. She came back to reality and started walking toward the restaurant. There was work to do.

The walk gave her a few moments to gather her thoughts. She needed to know who had a motive.

Maddie's cell phone rang as she stopped in front of Janet's. The sight of Dean's name surprised her. Wasn't he supposed to be sleeping?

# CHAPTER 12

"*M*om, he said I could call you."

"Who?" Maddie's heart pounded as she heard the panic in Dean's voice.

"There's a police officer here. I have to go with him."

"You most certainly do not. Don't you go anywhere with him! I'll be right there!" Maddie turned around to start back to the bakery where her car was parked.

"He's not asking, Mom. I don't have a choice."

"Everything's going to be okay. I'll sort this all out." As Maddie started back toward her car, she spotted a familiar vehicle in the parking lot. A police car with *Chief* stenciled on it. Determination took over as she turned back around, walked toward the door of the restaurant, and opened it.

When Maddie stepped inside, a familiar voice greeted her, before her eyes had a chance to adjust to the dimmer light.

"Maddie, I was just about to call you."

"Jake! How could you do this?" Maddie walked across the restaurant toward his table.

"Sit down." Jake gestured to the seat across from him.

"I'm not here to take orders." Maddie stood in front of him.

"Sit down, please." Jake looked up at her, then scanned the crowd in the restaurant. "You're making a scene."

"So?" Maddie crossed her arms. "I want everyone to know what you're up to. How could you send an officer to pick up Dean? You weren't even brave enough to show up yourself."

"Sit down." Jake used the tip of his shoe to nudge the chair out from the table. "I'm not discussing this, until you do."

"Fine." Maddie pulled the chair away from the table and sat down on it. "What happened to 'trust me, Maddie'?"

"What happened to me being able to trust you?"

Jake stared straight into her eyes. "How do you think it felt to be blindsided with information that you and Dean should have given me?"

"What information?" Maddie shook her head. "Dean is innocent. There's no information that changes that."

"Information that Dean had an argument with Ricardo not long before he was killed. Information, that I am certain, is not news to you." Jake's eyes bored into hers. "Whether or not he's innocent, withholding that kind of information is reason enough to take him in for questioning. If you had told me from the beginning, this wouldn't have happened."

"You never allowed me into the room when Dean was questioned. I didn't have the opportunity to tell you." Maddie's heart sank as she realized the truth in his words. Dean never should have kept the argument to himself. "He was just trying to protect me, Jake."

Jake sat back as Lacy approached their table.

"Shh." He held up his hand to Maddie as Lacy pulled out her notepad.

"What can I get for you two?"

"I'll have the bacon cheeseburger with a side of

fries, Lacy." Jake looked across the table at Maddie. "Go ahead and order."

Maddie tried to ignore the hunger pain that sent a cramp through her stomach. She hadn't eaten anything all morning.

"I should be on my way. I want to be there when Dean is released."

"Trust me, it's going to take a little while. We aren't done with our discussion." Jake glanced up at Lacy. "Just bring her the same order."

"Just a salad, please." Maddie cleared her throat.

"Coming right up." Lacy smiled at them both before hurrying away.

"How can you just sit here and order food as if you don't have a care in the world?" Maddie stared into his eyes. "My son is in your custody."

"Just for questioning." Jake took a sip of his water. "I'm here because I already know everything I need to know about Dean at the moment. I am going to talk to him again later. What I need now is new information. Sometimes that comes from being out in the public and listening in. Lucky for me, you just happened to drop in to join me for lunch. Now, tell me what you know about Ricardo."

"I don't know anything about him. I've told you

that. But what if he wasn't here to see me?" Maddie leaned forward. "Amber told me that he'd been seen around town, even before I moved back home. Obviously he'd had some other local connections."

"Unfortunately, he had a few too many." Jake looked up as Lacy returned with a plate and a large bowl in her hands. She set the salad down in front of Maddie, and the burger down in front of Jake.

Maddie's stomach growled at the sight and smell of the burger.

"Thanks." She managed a smile for Lacy as she walked away. When she looked back at Jake, the smile disappeared. "What do you mean he has too many?"

Jake took a bite of his burger, then set it down on his plate. He wiped his mouth with his napkin.

"I've had a difficult time narrowing down the suspects." He picked up the knife beside his plate and cut his burger into two halves.

"You already knew he wasn't here to see me?" Maddie narrowed her eyes. "Then why didn't you tell me that?"

"Just because there are other suspects, doesn't mean he wasn't planning on seeing you as well." Jake picked up one half of the burger that he hadn't had a bite out of and put it on top of Maddie's salad leaves.

The glossy bun of the burger caught her eye. The scent of the perfectly cooked meat wafted under her nose. Her mouth watered.

"Why did you do that?" Maddie's eyes widened as she stared at him.

"I know you don't want that salad." Jake pointed at her bowl. "Eat some real food."

"Grease, instead of nutritious vegetables?" Maddie quirked an eyebrow.

"Then you don't want it?" Jake reached for the burger.

"Leave it." Maddie's fingertips struck the back of his hand before he could touch it. Startled by her own reaction, she looked up at him, expecting some form of wrath.

Jake smiled as he gazed at her. "Go on, then. Eat up!"

"You're ridiculous, you know that?" Maddie picked up the burger and took a bite. The delicious flavor seeped across her taste buds, inspiring a quiet moan of appreciation.

"Am I?" Jake took another bite of his half. "I'm just looking out for you, making sure that you're well fed." He had a sip of water. "We're not going to get anywhere, if you don't start believing that we're on the same side here."

"I guess I just don't understand why." Maddie picked up her glass of water. "Why are we on the same side? Why are you being so kind to me? We could be down at the station right now. Instead, you're sharing your burger with me. Why?"

"Because I want to, Maddie." Jake slid his plate closer to her. "And some french fries, too."

"Thank you." Maddie snatched a fry from his plate.

"Right now, we need to focus on this crime. We need to focus on finding out what the locals know. Right?" Jake popped a fry in his mouth.

"Right." Maddie polished off the last bite of the burger. "But I haven't lived here in a long time. Most people don't even remember me."

"I doubt that." Jake sat back in his chair. "And if they don't, then you should make them. You know how this town works. Not much has changed over the years. You have connections that I never will. People always hold me at arm's length, due to my involvement in law enforcement. You, on the other hand, you're someone that anyone would be willing to talk to, gossip with. So, see what you can find out. Make sure you're careful, though. There is a murderer on the loose after all." He pointed to his plate. "Want to finish my fries?"

"I really shouldn't." Maddie eyed the fries.

"Why not?"

"I'm trying to eat healthier and lose some weight." Maddie's cheeks flushed as she glanced away from him.

Jake slid the plate closer to her.

"You don't need to change a single thing about you, Maddie." He stood up from the table and tossed down some cash to cover the bill. He slid his hat onto his head, then tipped it in her direction. "Keep me up to date." He started toward the door.

"What about his phone records?" Maddie followed after him. "Have you found out who he'd been in contact with recently?"

"We're going over them now. His phone was smashed when we found it, so we couldn't get any information directly from it." Jake pushed the door open. "Luckily, I have a pretty good tech guy at the station. Hopefully, he'll be able to get some information from it. Between that and the phone records, we should come up with something. Until then, you're the only expert I have on Ricardo."

"I'm no expert." Maddie stepped through the door that he held open for her.

"Maddie," Jake spoke softly. "I know why Craig was involved with him. I know why Dean felt the need to confront him, to protect you. I know you've had a few run-ins with Ricardo since you separated from Craig."

"Well, I guess you already know all the details, then, don't you?" Maddie stepped out from under his arm and turned to look at him. "What do you need me for?"

"I need you to tell me who Ricardo was." Jake maintained his distance as he studied her. "What did you see when you looked into his eyes?"

"What did I see?" Maddie stared back at him. "I saw a criminal. I saw a man that would do anything he could to make someone else miserable, in order to get what he wanted from them."

"Did you see a murderer?" Jake raised his eyebrows. "Were you frightened he would do more than threaten you?"

Maddie's heart skipped a beat as she recalled her last encounter with Ricardo. It had been in the dark, just after the movers had taken away the last of her possessions from the home she'd raised her children in. He cornered her near the garage door and promised her that she would regret not paying him.

"What did he say he would do to you?" Jake asked.

"I don't remember." Maddie crossed her arms and looked down at her feet.

"Maddie, the more you can tell me about his tactics, the more I can piece together what might have happened here." Jake's voice softened. "You don't have to be afraid to tell me anything."

"He told me, if I didn't start paying him back for what Craig owed him, he would go after my family." Maddie forced her eyes to his. "I couldn't let that happen."

Jake stared back at her for a long moment.

"So, what did you do?"

"I paid him. I gave him everything I had on hand and promised to give him more." Maddie sighed as she shook her head. "I wasn't brave. I wasn't strong. I just gave in to him. I don't know what that can tell you, but that's what happened."

"You did the only thing that you could, Maddie. You protected your family."

"Did I? It looks like he might have come back for more. I guess this makes me even more of a suspect."

"It does." Jake walked toward the parking lot. "And it also tells me that he used very threatening tactics to get what he wanted. Which means that he might have done the same to any number of people he interacted with." He scanned the sidewalk that stretched out in front of the restaurant, and farther along the harbor, toward the marina. "It tells me that anyone could have been angry enough to kill him, whether they had the money to pay him off or not." He opened the door to his car, then glanced back at her. "Thank you, Maddie, you've been very helpful." He hesitated a moment, then continued. "And I'm very sorry that happened to you."

"Thanks." Maddie watched as he settled in the driver's seat. As much as she wanted to understand more about him, the more time she spent with him, the more puzzling he became.

As Jake pulled out of the parking spot, her phone chimed. She read the text, then hurried to the bakery. Amber's mother, Iris, had information to share with her, and she was quite eager to hear it.

## CHAPTER 13

When Maddie reached the bakery, she rushed inside.

"Iris?" She peered around the dusty interior of the space. "Hello? Is anyone here?"

"In the kitchen!" Tammy's voice sang out.

Maddie pushed through the double doors that led to the kitchen. The whoosh of the doors as they swung shut behind her, reminded her of the thousands of times she'd heard the same sound before. So long ago, and yet it felt like the same moment.

"Just making some tea, dear." Iris filled a lime-green teakettle with water. "It's my good luck gift for the sale. I was going to give it to you for the bakery, if you decided to open it back up, but you can just take it home with you."

"Thank you so much, Iris." Maddie glanced over at Tammy and Amber, then looked back at Iris. "Can you please tell me what you know about Ricardo and what might have happened to him. Who might have killed him?"

"I can tell you who to look into first." Iris set the teakettle down on the burner, then turned to face the others. "Captain Niles."

"Captain Niles?" Maddie frowned as she recalled the boat tour she'd shared with Tammy and Dean the day before. "Why him?"

"His is one of the newer businesses in town." Iris grabbed a rag from beside the sink and began wiping off the faucet. "From what I hear, he got his business going very quickly, and no one knows exactly how."

"Maybe he received a grant?" Maddie glanced over at Amber. "He could have, right?"

"The people who receive it get an extensive background check. From what I understand, he didn't pass it." Amber pursed her lips. "My guess is, there was something fishy in his past."

"Fishy. Is that a pun?" Tammy grinned. "I mean, since he's a boat captain?" She glanced around at the others. "Get it?"

"Got it, Tammy." Maddie rolled her eyes as she laughed. "Well, if he was denied the grant, he had to get the money to start up from somewhere. I imagine it wasn't cheap to buy the boat, rent the space at the marina, and get all the permits and licenses he needed to run his business."

"Exactly," Iris agreed. "I'm sure he wasn't the only one to turn to Ricardo for help. I would think he would need a good reason to ask him for help, though. Also, you didn't hear it from me, but someone told me they saw the two of them in quite an argument early yesterday morning."

"Oh?" Maddie's eyes widened. "You should tell me who told you that, so I can tell the police. Or they should go to the police."

"That's not going to happen." Iris turned toward the teakettle as it began to whistle. "That's all the information that I can give you."

"All right, it's a start. Thank you so much, Iris. I can head over there and talk to him now." Maddie turned back toward the door.

"Maddie, I just got notification that the listing is up." Tammy followed after her to the front of the bakery. "Hopefully, it will sell quickly."

"Hopefully." Maddie glanced over her shoulder

at Tammy. "All I can really think about right now is making sure the murderer is found and Dean's name is cleared."

"Of course." Tammy nodded. "Well, whatever I can do to help, I'm here. Maybe I could go around town and gather up some gossip? I might be able to find out if Ricardo was loaning money to anyone else?"

"That would be great. Thank you." Maddie grabbed her purse from the front counter. "Let me know if you come across anything at all."

"I will!" Tammy's voice followed after her as she hurried to her SUV.

Minutes later, Maddie parked in one of the few reserved spots for Captain Niles' boat tours. She stepped out of the car and walked toward the boat. As she looked it over, she noted the newness of it and everything attached to it. She imagined it had to cost a lot. She noticed a clipboard perched on the edge of the boat and leaned closer to it in an attempt to get a look at what might be written on it.

"Ahoy there, matey!" Sam's rugged voice sounded from a few feet away.

Maddie jumped back from the clipboard as her heart raced.

"Back for more already?" Sam grinned as he

stood beside a plain, black cargo van and hefted a large crate into his arms. "I'm afraid there are no tours this afternoon."

"Actually, I'm not here for a tour. Although, I had a great time on the tour yesterday." Maddie watched as the muscles in his arms strained against the taut sleeves of his T-shirt. "I'm here because I'm thinking about opening my own business in town. I was told that you are one of the newest business owners. I thought maybe you could give me some tips on getting started?" She opened her purse. "I can pay you for your time." She pulled out her wallet. "Well, a little anyway."

Sam dropped the crate onto the boat, then descended the ramp back to the dock. "Opening a business, huh? It's not so easy in this town. They make it sound great, but it's tough to get started. What kind of business are you opening?"

Maddie took a second to answer. She hadn't prepared for the question, so she said the first thing that came to mind.

"A bakery. It's actually, more like reopening it. My parents used to run it when I was young." She scrunched up her nose. "I had no idea it would be so expensive."

"Phew, yes, that's going to cost you a lot to get

started. Have you tried for one of the business grants?" Sam wiped some sweat from his brow with the back of his hand. "It might help you get started."

"I'm afraid, I don't qualify." Maddie waved her hand. "Something about some issues in my past."

"Oh right. I had the same problem." Sam rolled his eyes. "I don't know why something that happened ten years ago should matter now, but it did."

"So, you couldn't get the grant, but you still managed to open your business?" Maddie looked over the boat. "It must have been so expensive for you."

"I had to get a little help." Sam nodded, then hesitated. "But I wouldn't recommend it."

"What do you mean? Please, you have to tell me how you did it. I don't want to give up, but I need some money to get started." Maddie searched his eyes. "Do you have any idea how I could get some?"

"Listen, there are always ways to get money. But some of the people that you have to deal with can be pretty shifty." Sam lowered his voice as he looked into her eyes. "It's not the way a lady like you should do things."

"Oh, don't let this flowery blouse fool you." Maddie gestured to the silky blouse she wore. "I can stand up for myself. I do what needs to be done. If there's a way to make this happen, I want to know about it."

"I'm sorry. I can't help you." Sam started to turn away from her. "I wish you luck, though."

Maddie watched him as he disappeared into the cabin. Part of her wanted to follow after him, and demand more of an answer, but she felt as if she'd already gotten all he would offer. Clearly, he had been involved with Ricardo, or someone like Ricardo. As she turned toward the parking lot, she caught sight of more crates stacked near the open doors of the van. Curious, she crept closer to the crates. She sank her fingers through the opening between two wooden slats in an attempt to discover what might be inside.

"Stop it!" The man's shout raised the hairs on the back of Maddie's neck. Had she been caught?

# CHAPTER 14

Maddie took a step back from the crates and looked in the direction of the shout.

Just across the street, she spotted a young couple, one of whom she recognized as the man who had been a bit rude to Lacy at Janet's Place yesterday. She recalled his name was Tim.

"What did you do?" Tim's voice raised as he stepped toward the woman in front of him.

"Nothing." The woman shook her head.

Tim's stance immediately put Maddie on edge.

"Hey!" Maddie's commanding voice cut through the din of the marina and made Tim freeze. "What's going on?" She marched toward him, as her protective instincts flared.

The woman moved farther away from Tim as Maddie neared them.

"Veronica, you need to listen to me." Tim stepped toward her again.

"No, you don't!" Maddie stepped boldly between the feuding pair.

"This is none of your concern." Tim shot a sharp glare in her direction, then attempted to step around her to reach Veronica.

"It absolutely is my concern." Maddie stepped to the side at the same time Tim did and blocked his path. "You have no business shouting at someone like that."

"She's not someone. She's my wife," Tim growled his words as he again attempted to dodge around her. "I just need to speak to her."

"You shouldn't shout at anyone like that. You are making such a commotion." Maddie glanced over her shoulder at Veronica, who stood with her arms wrapped around herself. "Are you okay, Veronica?"

"I'm fine, it's okay." Veronica smiled slightly. "We're just having a little disagreement. Tim never usually raises his voice in public. Don't worry about it."

"No?" Maddie looked over at Tim. "Because I

overheard him being quite rude to a waitress yesterday."

"I'm sorry." Tim held up his hands. "I can have a bit of a temper. We just got into a heated discussion, and I got a little too loud. I apologize." He looked past her at Veronica. "I'm sorry. Can you forgive me?"

"Yes, of course." Veronica waved her hand in the air. "It was nothing."

"Okay, as long as you're okay." Maddie turned toward Veronica. "I'm Maddie. I'm new to the area. I live just down the street. If you ever want to catch up, here's my number." She handed her a card.

"Thanks." Veronica looked over the card. "I remember seeing you around now. You have those two little dogs."

"Oh, yes. Bella and Polly."

"So cute." Veronica smiled.

"I have a business meeting. Lawson is already waiting for me at Janet's." Tim placed his hand on Veronica's arm. "We better get going."

Maddie watched them leave. She got the impression that Veronica had no intention of calling her.

As Maddie neared her car, her phone chimed in her pocket. Hoping it would be Dean saying that he had been released, she pulled it out and found a text from Tammy.

*We already have a good offer for the bakery.*

Maddie's heart fluttered with relief and then a hint of sadness.

After she settled in her car, she leaned her head back against the headrest and let her mind drift back over thirty years. Her childhood felt like another lifetime, but the moment her father's face came into focus, she snapped back into that time as if she'd never left. His warm smile, the excitement in his eyes.

"One day, Maddie, all of this will be yours." He held up his flour-covered hands and laughed.

In her teens, the thought of taking over the family business didn't excite her. She didn't want to be stuck in a little town, doing the same thing every day. Her heart sank as she recalled her response to him.

"It can all be Tammy's. I have other plans." Maddie had left the bakery without looking back once. Had she hurt her father's feelings? Now that she was a parent, she couldn't imagine how he wouldn't have been hurt. It was one of the last conversations she'd ever had with him.

"Oh, Dad, I would give anything to change that

moment." Maddie recalled the way they would argue. She'd always had an easier relationship with her mother. According to her mother, she and her father were too alike to get along. But as Maddie remembered it, he always wanted more from her. He doted on Tammy as the younger child, while assigning Maddie chores in the bakery every chance he got. Now, looking back on it, she guessed he was trying to prepare her for taking over the bakery. She felt a pang of sadness that they were actually selling it.

Maddie started the engine and drove back toward the house she'd grown up in. With Tammy waiting there for her, it felt like home.

As Maddie neared the house, she resisted the urge to turn in the other direction and head for the police station instead. The thought of Dean being interrogated by the police made her even more determined to solve this quickly and eliminate any chance that he could be arrested.

Maddie parked in the driveway and started to step out of the car. As she did, a dark blue sedan rolled slowly past the house. She tried to peer through the window to see who drove the car, but the dark tint on it prevented her from seeing anything. As the car crawled by, a shiver raced up her spine. Maybe the driver just wanted to get a look at the house. Maybe they had heard that Dean had been taken in for questioning. Maybe the driver was a local, curious about Maddie, and her move back to town. But the thought that played through her mind as she neared the front porch was much darker.

Maybe the driver was Ricardo's murderer. Maybe the murderer worried she might know too much. Her heart pounded at the thought. Had she seen more last night than she realized? Was there some clue she had overlooked? She paused on the front porch and closed her eyes. She pictured the walk she'd taken with the dogs, and the way they'd barked. She'd thought it was because they sensed Ricardo's body nearby. But what if it was the murderer that they had been barking at? Maybe she didn't see who killed Ricardo, but that didn't mean that the murderer hadn't seen her.

"You're being paranoid, Maddie." She sighed as she reached for the doorknob. As she turned it, she hoped that she might find her son on the other side. Maybe the police had already released him. Maybe he'd been waiting for her to get home.

Maddie whipped open the front door and rushed inside.

"Dean?" she called out.

Bella and Polly ran up to her, eager to be snuggled. She crouched down to rub behind their ears.

Maddie stood up and stepped farther into the house with the dogs at her heels.

"Dean, are you here?"

A sound of the fridge door closing in the kitchen drew her toward it.

# CHAPTER 15

ammy peeked out through the kitchen door.

"It's just me, Maddie. Sorry to disappoint." She held up a bottle of wine. "But I did pick up some refreshments for later."

"Dean isn't here?" Maddie leaned against the doorframe. "I had hoped the police would be done with him by now, but I haven't heard from him. What if they arrest him, Tammy?"

"Jake isn't going to let that happen." Tammy put the bottle down and poured coffee into two mugs.

"He can't stop an arrest. Dean didn't tell him about the argument he had with Ricardo, and somehow he found out about it. Now, Dean looks even more guilty." Maddie cringed.

"An argument doesn't make him guilty." Tammy set the coffeepot back down and turned to look at her sister. "Slow down. You'll have him locked up and convicted for life before you take your next breath. Focus on what we know. Dean is innocent. All we have to do is prove that."

"True." Maddie gazed at her sister. "We just have to concentrate on getting this thing solved."

"Did you find out anything from Captain Niles?" Tammy handed her a coffee.

"Thank you." Maddie took the mug. "He basically admitted that he had help to get his business off the ground, and from the way he put it, he's involved with some dangerous people. He didn't say it was Ricardo, though." She sat down on the couch and thought back over their conversation. "He really didn't tell me too much. But I do know that he's doing something other than boat tours. He was moving large crates onto his boat. I almost got a look inside of them."

"You didn't, though?" Tammy sat down beside her.

Bella and Polly jumped up onto the couch between them.

Bella perched her paws on Maddie's leg and looked up at her.

Polly snuggled into Tammy's side.

"I didn't, because I was distracted." Maddie rubbed behind Bella's ear. "Tim, the guy from the restaurant yesterday, that was rude to Lacy, he was arguing with his wife at the marina. He was quite loud."

"Oh? Did you get the details?" Tammy grinned. "Good gossip is like gold around here."

"I didn't, really." Maddie put down the coffee cup. "But I did make sure they were okay."

"Maddie, did you really get in the middle of it?" Tammy covered her mouth as she gasped.

"I did." Maddie nodded. "You would have done the same thing."

"I hope I would have." Tammy bit into her bottom lip. "What happened?"

"They insisted it was just a disagreement and they stopped arguing. So, I left it at that."

"Oh, when I spoke to Frances at Flowers by Frances, she mentioned something about Tim and Veronica." Tammy sat forward.

"She did?"

"Yes, apparently Veronica and Frances are friends. Veronica was all upset because Tim didn't have the funds to support the amusement park build, and Lawson, his business partner, was thinking about pulling out. Lawson had been helping fund the build, but he was getting frustrated by the delays. She didn't tell me more than that."

"Interesting. I wonder if it means anything." Maddie had a sip of coffee. "Tim and Lawson seemed to have a disagreement at Janet's yesterday."

"Oh, that's right." Tammy clicked her fingers. "I remember now, but I don't know what it was about."

"Me, neither. I sent a text to a friend of mine. She's a police officer and a good friend. I helped her look into someone who was scamming her. So, she was prepared to help me. I asked her to see if she can get Ricardo's phone records from around the time of the murder." Maddie held the mug between both palms. "She said she'll try."

"Oh, good idea." Tammy placed her mug down on the table. "Hopefully, she comes through for you."

"She should. But it doesn't mean there is anything relevant there."

"So, we really are selling the bakery." A hint of sadness glazed Tammy's eyes.

"Looks like it."

"Are you sure you don't want to open it?" Tammy looked over at her.

"It's just not practical." Maddie ran her hand along Bella's back.

"I know, I know, I'm just being crazy Tammy again." She swallowed the remainder of her coffee.

"I don't think you're crazy, Tammy." Maddie looked into her eyes. "I just think sometimes we have to look at the practical side of things. I don't have the money to run the place. I don't have the skills. I've barely made cupcakes lately. In fact, I've only made them once since Craig and I separated. When I first got here."

"Seriously?" Tammy stared back at her.

"I just haven't felt like it." Maddie shrugged. "And I'm trying to be healthier." She gave a short laugh as she realized it barely ever worked.

"Oh, Maddie, you come alive when you bake." Tammy took her hand and clasped it tight. "You need to do the things you love."

"Tammy, it's really not that big of a deal." Maddie shrugged again. "I've just lost interest, I guess."

"Okay, that's it, we're going straight to the kitchen." Polly hopped down out of Tammy's lap as she stood up.

Bella followed after her as Tammy pulled Maddie to her feet.

"Tammy, this is silly. This isn't the time for me to be baking anything." Maddie tried to pull her hand free.

"It absolutely is, and we're not doing anything else until you do." Tammy tightened her grip on her hand and tugged her toward the kitchen.

"Tammy!" Maddie rolled her eyes. "I don't have time for this. I need to focus on who killed Ricardo."

"If you stop thinking about it so much, things will become clearer for you." Tammy released her hand and fished her phone out of her pocket. "You need to remember who you are!" She set the phone on the counter, and moments later music played through it.

"Tammy, no," Maddie groaned as the music filled the kitchen.

"Start twisting." Tammy began dancing in her sister's direction.

"Not now." Maddie marched toward the living room.

Tammy caught her around the waist and pulled her back to the center of the kitchen.

"Oh, you don't remember how? I'll show you!" She grabbed her hips and began wiggling them.

Maddie burst into laughter as she gave in to her sister's insistence and began moving her hips to the music. Her mind filled with memories of her parents dancing together in the kitchen, while teaching their daughters the dance as well.

"Oh, you have to go lower than that." Tammy squealed as she crouched down and swung her hips.

"Are you going to pick me up off the floor?" Maddie grinned and inched just a little lower.

"Always." Tammy winked at her as she began shifting her feet back and forth. "Don't act like you don't know how to shake it!"

"Tammy, this is ridiculous! Dean is with the police!" Maddie tried to ignore her sister's antics.

"And you dancing a little won't do any harm!" Tammy twisted her way down to a crouch. "It will help clear your head, and maybe you'll be able to help him more."

Maddie sighed and relented. She felt her mind shift from all of her concerns to the rhythm of the music, and her body began to follow along. A sense of joy surfaced as she danced with her sister.

"Now, you're ready to make cupcakes." Tammy grinned as she grabbed her hands. "Let's get started."

# CHAPTER 16

For a few minutes, Maddie lost herself in the process of gathering all the ingredients she would need. Ever since her mother taught her the recipe at ten years old, she had been making raspberry cupcakes for special celebrations. She'd made many other kinds of cupcakes as well, but the first recipe her mother taught her, always remained her favorite.

As Maddie rummaged through the same cabinets, and set the ingredients out on the same counter, her heart filled with warmth as the happy memories came flooding back. She began combining the ingredients into a large bowl, while Tammy made sure the tunes kept playing and continued to dance around the kitchen.

Maddie grabbed a scoop of flour to add to the mix.

Tammy spun in her direction and knocked the flour out of the scoop and into the air.

"Oh, no!" Maddie gasped as the flour burst upward into the air, then showered down all over her.

At the same time, a knock sounded on the front door, then it swung open.

"Mom, I'm home," Dean's voice carried through the house.

Maddie forgot about the flour peppered through her dark hair and splashed across the front of her blouse. She bolted toward the front door just in time to see Jake step in after Dean.

"Mom?" Dean looked her over with a dazed smile. "What happened to you?"

"It doesn't matter. I'm so happy to see you!" Maddie threw her arms around him and hugged him tight.

"Mom, you're getting flour all over me." Dean laughed as he pulled away from her.

Tammy hurried over to Maddie with a dish towel. "I'm sorry, Maddie, I didn't mean to bump into you."

Jake settled his gaze on Maddie, then glanced

away as a faint smile crossed his lips.

Maddie noticed the quick look and smile and became very aware of her messy appearance.

"We were making cupcakes." Tammy dabbed the dish towel against Maddie's blouse. "It was my idea. When your mom told me that she barely bakes anymore, in fact, only once since she's been here, I just knew she had to get baking."

"Really?" Dean looked at his mother. "You always loved baking, making cupcakes. You said it made you feel like a magician."

"Well, obviously, cupcakes aren't my friend right now." Maddie laughed nervously as she dusted some flour off her hands. "Aunt Tammy was just trying to distract me, because I was worried about you."

"I'm all right, Mom." Dean glanced over at Jake.

"I told you I'd take care of him." Jake crossed his arms as he looked her over. "I hate to interrupt the magic, but I do need to speak with you."

"It's fine, absolutely fine." Maddie forced a smile as she wished that all of the flour would suddenly disappear. She looked over at Dean. "Go on in the kitchen, Aunt Tammy has some coffee ready. I'm sorry I wasn't here to stop the police."

"There's nothing you could have done." Dean

paused. "I should have listened to you, and told Jake about the argument, then none of this would have happened."

"You did what you thought was best, Dean. I'm going to take care of all of this. Okay?" Maddie patted his arm. "You believe me, don't you?"

"You're the magician, Mom." Dean kissed her cheek, then followed Tammy into the kitchen.

A bit flustered, Maddie turned back to face Jake.

"Are you satisfied now? Do you see that he's innocent?"

"Maddie, I'd love to tell you that Dean is no longer on our suspect list. But the truth is, he doesn't have an alibi. He was seen arguing with the victim, and he has a good motive for wanting to get rid of him." Jake's voice remained even. "And that's not all."

"What do you mean, 'that's not all'?" Maddie heard the sharpness in her own tone. "What else could there possibly be? He didn't kill Ricardo!"

"I'm not saying that he did, Maddie. He was treated fairly. Of course. But there's nothing I can do about the fact that they found Dean's sunglasses beside Ricardo's body. When Dean was asked about it, he claimed he was never in the area where Ricardo was murdered. He said that he must have lost his sunglasses and didn't even realize they were missing until we mentioned it." Jake raised his eyebrows. "Do you really think someone can lose their sunglasses without noticing?"

"Obviously, yes. If that's what Dean said, then that's what happened." Maddie crossed her arms as her heart raced. "He's innocent."

Jake stepped toward her and lowered his voice.

"The only reason Dean is back home is because I made the decision not to hold him. We have evidence against him, and the investigation is ongoing. He could still be arrested at any time, and he needs to stay in the area. Do you understand that?"

"I do." Maddie noticed the way his expression softened. "Jake, he didn't do this."

"So you say. But I need to find out if that's true. So, help me." Jake met her eyes. "You can start by telling me about your interaction out at the marina today."

"At the marina?" Maddie wondered how he could know about that.

"Someone noticed you talking to Tim and Veronica today. He said they were having a shouting match, and you went to talk to them, probably to calm things down."

"Really? I didn't see anyone else around. Who was it?" Maddie searched through her memory of those moments.

"I'd rather not name my sources." Jake's tone became indifferent.

"Were you having me followed, Jake?"

"Why would I have you followed?" Jake glanced toward the kitchen. "Why would you think that?"

"Because you still think I'm a suspect." Maddie's heart skipped a beat as she detected the cologne he wore. The fact that he was quite close, distracted her. But why? "I don't have an alibi, either, and I have plenty of motive. My dogs were heard in the area, and my fingerprints were at the scene."

"I don't think you're a suspect." Jake leaned against the wall beside her. "I never did. I told you that."

"That's just what you said to con me." Maddie took a step back, away from him. "I can't pretend that I don't believe that the police suspect me and my son. I have to do something to clear my name, my son's name."

"Con? Maddie, I asked you to trust me." Jake

crossed his arms. "And I've given you every reason to do just that. I'm not playing any games. I'm trying to solve this crime. Are you so determined to believe I'm trying to con you that you'll risk your son's freedom to prove it?"

"Is everything okay out here?" Tammy popped her head out of the kitchen and looked between the two of them.

"Just fine, Tammy," Maddie called out.

Maddie knew she had to do what she could to make it seem as if she was Jake's ally, even if she wasn't sure he was hers. He was her best chance to clear Dean's name.

*a*s Tammy disappeared back into the kitchen, Maddie turned toward Jake. "Of course, I'll help you, Jake. In any way that I can." She smiled. "Are you looking into another possible suspect? Captain Niles?"

"Did you find out something about him?"

"I spoke with him today about how he gathered the funds to start his business, since he didn't qualify for any of the grants available. He indicated that he had to get the money from a dangerous source. I am willing to bet that it was Ricardo, but I can't prove that, yet. I will, though." Maddie's voice grew stern. "That makes him a pretty good suspect, in my book."

"It does, does it? Anything else?" Jake asked.

"I think he's up to something. I saw him loading crates onto his boat."

"Many of the captains that give tours also do some transport runs in their off times." Jake met her eyes. "Is there any reason to think that what he's doing is illegal?"

"Not necessarily. I was going to take a look inside one of the crates, when I heard Tim and Veronica arguing. I just wanted to check they were okay. They were making quite a scene."

"Maddie, you can't go snooping around like that." Jake shook his head. "You can keep your eyes and ears open, but you shouldn't go taking risks like that. You need to be careful."

"I am being careful." Maddie considered telling him about the car that rolled past her house. But she decided against it. It was probably nothing. "I know that you probably could have arrested Dean today with the evidence you found."

"I'm not interested in arresting anyone but the murderer." Jake reached up and brushed some flour from her hair. The gesture surprised her.

As flour drifted in the air between them, she looked into his green eyes. She found a surprising warmth beyond the professional authority he wielded.

"Like I said, I appreciate what you're doing for Dean, and I'll help in any way that I can."

Jake's hand settled back to his side as he took a step back from her. "I'll be in touch."

"Thanks, Jake." Maddie watched him walk to the door and step out of the house.

As he left, Maddie's phone beeped with a text. It was from Justine, the police officer she knew from back home. It detailed that Ricardo had received calls from both Tim and Sam within about twenty minutes before his death. It also explained that as she had thought, Sam had a criminal history.

As Maddie put away her phone, Dean stepped out of the kitchen.

"Dean, are you okay?" Maddie asked.

"Fine." Dean held up his cup of coffee. "I'm going to drink this and pretend none of it ever happened." He waved to her as he climbed the stairs that led to his room.

A moment later, the front door opened.

Iris swept inside, her colorful dress swirling around her as she rushed toward Maddie.

"Darling! I just heard about Dean being questioned. Don't worry, I'm here!" She pulled Maddie into a tight hug.

Amber stepped in behind her mother.

Maddie barely noticed as the warm hug from Iris threatened to melt her into a puddle. She had no idea how much she needed that embrace, until it had surrounded her. She pulled away, and Iris dusted flour from her dress.

"I'm okay. Dean is home. Everything's fine." Maddie smiled.

"Don't you lie to me." Iris clucked her tongue as she led her into the kitchen. "Tell me what's happening, sweetheart." She pushed her toward the kitchen table.

"Why don't you finish baking while we talk, Maddie. The batter is halfway done." Tammy pointed to the bowl. "You've always loved whipping up something sweet. Remember what we were taught. Eating a sweet treat is enjoyable, but baking a sweet treat is comfort. It repairs the soul."

"She's not wrong, Maddie." Amber smiled. "Even when we were young, you and Tammy always made the best desserts for the bake sales. I always thought they tasted better, because you had so much fun making them."

Maddie stared across the kitchen at the bowl on the counter, and the ingredients that surrounded it. She felt a tiny spark in the middle of her chest at the thought of making a batch of cupcakes for everyone to enjoy.

"Come, let me help you." Iris walked over to the bowl. "You don't mind if I add a few of my own ingredients, do you? Maybe some cinnamon? How about some chocolate chips?" She grabbed a bottle of cinnamon and popped open the lid.

"Don't!" Maddie took a step toward her, her eyes wide. "You can't put cinnamon in raspberry cupcakes. It'll ruin the flavor. Chocolate chips will make them far too sweet and change the entire texture of the cupcake."

Iris smiled as she set the bottle of cinnamon down. "It sounds like you have a few things to show me about making cupcakes." She pushed the bowl toward her. "Go right ahead. I'll watch."

Maddie relaxed the moment the bottle of cinnamon hit the counter. Her mind swirled with the ingredients she would need to make the cupcakes a perfect balance between moist and spongy.

# CHAPTER 18

*A*s Maddie sifted the remainder of the flour, her muscles came alive with the memories of doing the same thing so many times before. The tiny spark returned, and grew, until it had warmed her entire body.

Amber shared a high five with Tammy as they watched.

"I wish Katie was here." Maddie smiled at the thought of Tammy's daughter. She often spent the summers at Maddie's house, and like her aunt and mother, she had a passion for baking. She recently finished her course at culinary school and was working at a bakery. "I miss baking with her."

"Oh, I also wish she was here." Tammy's voice

grew wistful. "You two always had so much fun together. She loved summer vacation with you."

Iris settled into a seat at the table and smiled.

"All right, while you work, let's figure this mess out. Tell me what we know so far." She patted the table with her palm. "We're going to get it all straightened out."

"We know that Dean is innocent." Tammy sat down across from her.

"And we know that it was most likely a local who killed Ricardo." Amber sat down beside Tammy.

"We do?" Maddie glanced over at her. "How? I imagine Ricardo had a lot of enemies. Maybe one of them followed him here?"

"If there had been a stranger in town, we would have heard about it." Amber paused. "No, I think it was a local."

"Wait, there was a man arguing with Sam right after we took the tour. Remember, Tammy?" Maddie added the sugar to the mixture.

"Yes, he didn't look like a friendly guy, that's for sure."

"What did he look like?" Iris glanced between them.

"Big, huge. Bushy eyebrows." Maddie rattled off the best description of what she could recall.

"Oh, that's Alex." Iris rolled her eyes. "He's more muscle than brain, for sure. He tries to pass himself off as a security guard, but everybody knows what he does."

"What does he do?" After adding the last ingredient and mixing just enough, Maddie spooned the batter into cupcake liners.

"He's hired muscle." Iris crossed her arms. "As far as I can tell, he goes around threatening people to do what whoever hires him wants."

"Really?" Tammy stared at her. "Right here in town? I wouldn't think that kind of thing went on around here."

"It's picked up quite a bit, since all the new buildings have been going up. The wealthy owners don't have any patience. They want the work done as quickly as possible, and the locals that are scrambling for the scraps, are doing what they can to protect what they have. It's made things pretty tense." Iris winced. "From what I heard, the amount of money changing hands behind closed doors is definitely out of control."

"The way he spoke to Sam made me think that he was angry about something." Maddie slid the cupcakes into the oven, then turned to face Iris. "Sam seemed a little scared of him."

"Sam isn't as tough as he looks. He's always trying to convince people that he's intimidating, but if you have to convince people, then you're not so intimidating, are you?" Iris chuckled. "If Alex was after Sam, then it probably wasn't for pleasant reasons."

"I think he borrowed money from Ricardo to start his business." Maddie sat down at the table with the others. "Do you think that Ricardo might have hired Alex to collect from Sam?"

"That would explain why Ricardo brushed Dean off." Tammy's eyes widened. "Maybe he really wasn't here to collect anything from you, Maddie. Maybe he was here to collect from Sam."

"If that's the case, then Sam definitely had good reason to want to go after Ricardo." Maddie's heartbeat quickened as excitement built within her. Maybe she had discovered the murderer after all. "But the problem is, I have to find a way to prove that. I need more information. Do you know if Sam is friends with anyone in town? Anyone that he might have confided in?"

"I've seen him talking to Tim and Lawson

several times." Amber sniffed the air. "Oh, those cupcakes smell amazing."

"They do." Maddie walked over to the oven. She paused beside it, then turned back to the table. "What is the relationship between Tim and Lawson? I heard them having a heated discussion at Janet's yesterday. Lawson isn't from around here, is he?"

"No, but he visits often." Amber leaned forward. "More and more often lately. Tim and Lawson have formed a partnership and are helping fund the building of the amusement park."

"I don't know much about them. All I know is that Lawson seems to have his hands in a lot of businesses in town, he's made a lot of connections here." Iris tapped the counter. "Tim was born here, but he has only really become involved in the businesses quite recently."

"Tim and his wife were at the marina today, arguing. What if somehow Tim was involved in Ricardo's murder? Or maybe Sam confessed to Tim he was involved in the murder? Or maybe Tim and Sam were in on it together? Maybe Tim and Veronica were arguing about it?" Maddie suggested.

"I guess that's all possible." Tammy looked up at the ceiling and tilted her head from side to side. "But it's also a stretch. They could have been arguing about anything, really. Even if it's true, how would you get Tim to tell you anything? I don't want you anywhere near that hothead."

"I don't know, yet, especially after I interrupted their argument today. But I have to figure it out." Maddie opened the oven, releasing a sweet raspberry scent. "I think they are ready. Just need to let them cool." She pulled the pan out of the oven and placed it on a cooling rack.

"They smell so good, they probably don't even need frosting." Amber licked her lips.

"Maybe not, but they'll definitely burn your tongue right now!" Tammy winced.

"Oh, where has the time gone." Iris looked at the clock. "I better get going. I have ballroom dancing tonight." She winked.

"And I need to give her a lift." Amber laughed.

"Why don't you come over in the morning and we can have cupcakes and pick up where we left off," Tammy suggested.

"That sounds wonderful." Iris smiled. "Thank you."

"It will have to be late-morning because I am working first thing at the grocery store," Amber said. "Is that okay?"

"Yes, I have some bookkeeping work to do in

the morning." Maddie and Tammy walked Amber and Iris to the car.

"We'll see you tomorrow." Tammy waved as they drove down the driveway. "How about we forget about this mess with Ricardo for a few hours. Let's watch a movie and have dinner with Dean?" She looped her arm around Maddie's as they headed back to the house. "We aren't going to solve anything more tonight. And I want you to enjoy some time with your son, and me of course."

"Sounds good," Maddie agreed. As much as she wanted the murder solved, she knew Tammy was right.

# CHAPTER 19

The following morning, Maddie woke to the dogs stirring beside her. She opened her eyes and gasped when she looked at the clock.

"Oh no. I've overslept."

The previous evening, she had made a chicken casserole, one of Dean's favorite childhood meals. By the time they had finished dinner and watched a movie, it was quite late. Despite the events of the last couple of days, she was so happy to have some time to spend with Dean and Tammy.

She remembered that Amber and Iris were joining them for cupcakes later that morning and she had a few hours of work to do first. She quickly got dressed. After feeding the dogs and having breakfast with Dean and Tammy, she started working. It took a lot longer than usual, because she was distracted by trying to figure out who had murdered Ricardo. When she was finished work she took the butter and cream cheese out of the fridge to get to room temperature, then she took the dogs for a walk.

When she came back, Amber and Iris were already at the kitchen table and Tammy was preparing coffee.

"Hi, Maddie." Iris looked up at her. "We're ready to solve this mystery. And we're ready for a delicious cupcake. Or two." She laughed.

"I'll get the frosting started." Maddie walked over to the mixer. "I haven't had time to frost them, yet."

"Hi, girls." Amber stood up and crouched down to greet the dogs.

"Okay, let's get back to figuring this out. Thank you." Iris smiled as Tammy put a cup of coffee down in front of her. "Where were we up to yesterday?"

"Tim and Veronica's argument and what it might have been about." Tammy had a sip of coffee.

"Okay, let's play this out." Amber stood up. "If Sam is the one who killed Ricardo, where is their connection? Maddie, you think he borrowed money from Ricardo? What makes you think that?"

"He didn't say any names, but he indicated that the person who gave him the funds for his business was dangerous." Maddie paused as she tried to recall his exact words. "At least I think that's what he said." She added cream cheese and butter to a mixing bowl.

"Okay, so if we assume that he did borrow the money from Ricardo, and that Alex showed up to collect from him, then we can guess that Sam refused to pay him. Maybe he met up with Ricardo later under the guise of making a payment, then he decided to kill him instead," Amber suggested. "Do we have any evidence to prove that?"

"A friend managed to get Ricardo's phone records for me, and apparently Sam called Ricardo not long before he was killed." Maddie added the confectioners' sugar, then turned on the mixer. She moved closer to them, away from the noise of the mixer. "It's not exactly evidence, but it does show a connection, and Sam could have been asking to meet up with him."

"Or, he could have been telling him to buzz off." Iris tapped her finger on the counter. "If he planned to kill him, why call him? Why not just sneak up on him?"

"True. And maybe Sam isn't the only one in

town that would profit from Ricardo being dead."
Tammy stood up from the table. "Is the frosting
ready?"

"Yes. Want to help?" Maddie smiled as she
picked up the bowl of cream cheese frosting.

"Do you trust me not to eat it all?" Tammy
laughed as she grabbed a spatula.

"Oh, I'll be watching." Maddie pretended to
glare at her sister. She loved being surrounded by
people she cared about. Instead of trying to piece
together what happened to Ricardo all on her own,
it felt as if she had an entire team to support her.

"I can't tell you how warm it makes my heart to
see you girls baking together." Iris sat back in her
chair as she watched them frost the cupcakes. "Your
parents would be so thrilled. It broke your mother's
heart when she had to shut down the bakery after
your father died."

"It did?" Maddie looked over at her. "I always
thought it was a relief for her to shut the place
down. Why else would she have closed it?"

"She had no choice. She didn't have the funds to
keep it going. It was either close the bakery down or
sell the house. She couldn't bring herself to sell the
house, she wouldn't have gotten much for it,
anyway. So, she boarded up the bakery and got a

job in town. Did you really think she wanted to be a secretary?" Iris raised her eyebrows.

"Yes." Maddie began placing a raspberry on top of each of the cupcakes.

"No." Tammy frosted the last cupcake, then looked up at Maddie. "Mom wasn't the type of person who wanted to be stuck in a pencil skirt behind a desk in a stuffy office. But she did it because she needed to keep a roof over our heads."

"I thought she loved the job." Maddie stared into her sister's eyes. "How did I miss all of this?"

"You were so devastated when Dad died." Tammy began piling the dirty dishes into the sink. "All you could talk about was getting away. You probably just didn't notice."

"I guess I didn't." Maddie wiped down the counter. "I thought I knew Mom so well."

"You did, sweetheart. You knew she loved you, and she did everything she could for you." Iris stood up and walked over to her. "That's what she wanted you to know." She patted her arm. "I'm sure that you've learned over the years, women can be really good at keeping secrets and putting on a show for everyone. Don't misunderstand me, your mother was happy. She was grateful she had the two of you, and she loved you both very much. But she didn't just lose your father when he passed, she lost her way of life, her business."

"Women are really good at keeping secrets," Maddie repeated Iris' words. "You're right. We try to make things look better than they are." She recalled the many times she brushed off Craig's absence as nothing to be concerned about, meanwhile she felt less and less important in his life. "That's it!" She suddenly straightened up. "I need to talk to Veronica again. If Tim has something to hide, she'll know about it." She grabbed a container from a nearby cabinet. "I'm going to go see her right now."

"Do you want company?" Amber asked.

"No, but thank you. If we both go, she might not be willing to tell me Tim's secret. If he has one, that is. If it's just me, I might be able to convince her." Maddie put some cupcakes in the container, careful not to mess the frosting. "Hopefully, she'll be willing to tell me whatever secrets he's been keeping."

"Good luck." Tammy turned on the faucet. "But don't expect there to be any cupcakes left when you get back."

"Don't worry, I'll save you one." Iris laughed as Maddie hurried to the door.

Bella and Polly chased after her.

"All right, all right. You can come with me." Maddie remembered that Veronica had mentioned the dogs. She probably wouldn't mind Maddie bringing them with, and might even want to meet them. Maddie juggled the cupcakes as she gathered their leashes, then herded them to the car. "But no trying to lick the frosting!"

She set the cupcakes down on the passenger seat and helped the dogs onto the back seat of her SUV. As she started the car, she wondered if the cupcakes would be enough. She hoped that bringing the dogs with might help get Veronica to talk to her. That was if she was even home. What would she do if Tim was there? She would deal with it then. She drove toward Veronica's house and rehearsed what she might say to her.

"Why did your husband call Ricardo? What business did he have with him? Does he have business with Sam Niles?" As the questions filled the car, Maddie shook her head. "I can't sound like I'm interrogating her."

Polly barked from the back seat.

"I know, I know. You catch more flies with honey, right, Polly?" Maddie reached back to pet her. Polly was always the louder and cheekier out of the two. She always wanted to get in the thick of things and lead the way.

Bella licked her hand.

As Maddie neared Tim's sprawling house, she reminded herself that Dean's future might depend on what information she could get from this woman. She needed to try and get the truth from her. She parked in the long driveway, then helped the dogs out of the car. Holding their leashes with one hand, she grabbed the container of cupcakes with the other hand.

"You two need to be good." Maddie looked at the dogs, then headed for the house. She noticed Veronica on her front porch. "Hi, Veronica."

"Maddie, right?" Veronica stepped to the end of the porch. "Oh, you brought the dogs. Aren't they gorgeous?" She walked down the steps and bent down to pet Bella and Polly, who eagerly wagged their tails.

"Oh, they like you. I brought you some cupcakes. They're raspberry with cream cheese frosting. I hope you like them." Maddie lifted up a corner of the lid to show her.

"They smell delicious." Veronica took the container from her. "But why did you bring me these?"

"I thought your day might need brightening." Maddie smiled. "I remember having disagreements with my ex-husband, and it always upset me. I just wanted to make sure you were okay after your argument."

"It was so embarrassing. I'm sorry you had to witness it."

"You have nothing to be sorry for. But I thought maybe you could use a listening ear."

Veronica placed the container on a chair near the bottom of the steps, then turned toward the dogs. She patted them as they strained on the end of their leashes to get to her.

"Is that why you came here, to get the gossip?"

"Not at all. I'm not one to gossip. I don't mean to pry. If you want me to go, I will. I just really can't shake the feeling that there was more to the argument, and you might want to talk about it. I just wanted to offer a friendly ear."

"Tim was just angry." Veronica crouched down and ruffled the fur on the dogs' heads. "And actually, he had a right to be. I made a really stupid choice, and it cost us both a lot. If I had been in his shoes, I probably wouldn't have shown as much restraint as he did."

"It sounds like you really trust him."

"I do. He's always been there for me. He's always walked this very thin line between two worlds. He grew up very poor, and now he deals with all of these wealthy and well-connected businessmen. A lot of them aren't always very forgiving." Veronica stood up. "It can be really stressful for him, but I'm very proud of him. It just takes a lot to keep up with everything."

"It's a good thing he has you to keep him grounded." Maddie paused, then lowered her voice. "Still, the way he was acting at the marina, it seemed like he was so upset. What mistake could you have made to get him so worked up?"

"I thought I was being helpful, but I wasn't. I try to stay out of his business, but he's been so stressed lately that I just wanted to make things easier for him, but I ended up doing the opposite." Veronica winced. "It's in the past now. That's all that matters."

"Is his business a little dangerous?" Maddie narrowed her eyes. "That might explain why he was so upset."

"It can be, I guess." Veronica glanced back at the house. "He doesn't tell me too much about it. But he deals with a lot of powerful men, and a lot of money. I guess that can be dangerous any time."

"Especially with him rubbing elbows with men

like Ricardo." Maddie shook her head. "I wouldn't want someone like that as my friend."

"Ricardo?" Veronica's tone suddenly shifted. "What are you talking about? Tim wasn't friends with Ricardo."

"He wasn't? I'm sure I saw the two of them together." Maddie hadn't seen them together, but she couldn't tell her that she knew Tim had called Ricardo shortly before his murder.

"You certainly didn't. Tim is a professional. He would never interact with a criminal like Ricardo." Veronica crossed her arms as she studied Maddie. "Why would you even think that?"

"Like I said, I thought I saw them together." Maddie tried to keep her voice even. "But I must have been mistaken."

"You were." Veronica patted the dogs' heads, then picked up the cupcakes. "Thanks for these. I'll be sure to share them with Tim." She climbed the steps toward her front door.

Maddie watched until she disappeared into the house. As she walked down the driveway toward her car with the dogs at her side, she wondered if Veronica really had no idea about her husband's connection to Ricardo, or if she had a good reason to lie about it.

# CHAPTER 20

*a*s Maddie neared her car, Bella and Polly started barking loudly and pulled to the ends of their leashes.

"What are you two upset about?" She looked around the wide lawn of the property. She didn't see anything that would grab the dogs' attention among the well-manicured grass.

"Settle down, please!" Maddie pulled her keys out of her pocket. As she did, she saw someone at the side of the driveway. The dogs kept barking in the man's direction.

"Oh, aren't they making a racket." The man dressed in coveralls and a large sun hat took a slight step back away from the dogs.

"I'm sorry, I don't know what's gotten into

them." Maddie noticed the dogs both crouched low and growled as they looked up at the man. "I'm Maddie. I just recently moved back into town. I'm sorry, I don't think we've met."

"Chip." He frowned as he looked down at the dogs. "Not very friendly, are they?"

"Normally, they are." Maddie looked past him, at a van parked along the road, with a sign that advertised his gardening business. "Do you have a card? I might need your services soon."

"Sure." Chip dug out a battered wallet and fished a business card from it. He handed it to her, then tipped his head toward the dogs. "They're noisy, aren't they?"

"They can be, but not usually." Maddie tucked the card into her pocket. "Thanks so much. I'll be calling you soon." She turned at the sound of a car pulling up at the end of the driveway. The man who stepped out of the dark blue SUV looked familiar to her. He adjusted his suit jacket as he walked toward them.

"Hey, Lawson." Chip waved to him.

"Chip." Lawson smiled, then he looked over at Maddie as he squinted. "I recognize you from Captain Niles' tour, I think?" He snapped his fingers. "You got off as I was boarding?"

"Yes, that's right." Maddie smiled as she tried to speak over the barking dogs. "Quiet down."

"Oh, they certainly are full of energy, aren't they?" Lawson held out his hand to her. "Lawson Foster."

"Maddie Mills. It's nice to meet you." Maddie shook his hand as the dogs continued to bark. "I better get them to the car. The neighbors will call the police, if they don't quiet down."

"Probably. This is a peaceful neighborhood." Lawson smiled as he started toward the house, and she continued down the driveway.

As Maddie drove back toward her house, she went over the conversation she'd had with Veronica. Was there something she might have missed? Some clue that would confirm Tim had killed Ricardo?

Maddie turned into her driveway. Despite her best efforts, she didn't have any good news for Dean. She wanted to be able to tell him that he no longer had to worry. As she stepped out of the car, Bella and Polly jumped out as well.

"You two were way too noisy." Maddie shooed them up onto the porch.

"Why were they noisy?" Tammy stood up from the rocking chair she had been sitting on.

"Oh, I don't know." Maddie walked up the

stairs. "They saw Veronica's gardener as I was leaving and they went crazy." She sat down on the other rocking chair. "The whole excursion was rather pointless. All I know is that she either lied to me or doesn't have a clue what her husband is up to."

"What did she lie about?" Tammy sat back down. Polly jumped up into her lap and curled into a fluffy ball.

"She claimed that Tim has no connection to Ricardo, but Tim called Ricardo not long before he was killed. So, he obviously has a connection to him. Why else would he call him at that hour?"

"That's a good point." Tammy rocked forward in her chair and cuddled Polly close to her. "But you're right, it doesn't get us any closer to solving the murder. What next?"

"I honestly have no idea. I'm feeling a little lost about it all. I think Tim could be involved, but I also think that Sam might be up to something underhanded." Maddie looked over at Bella who was running around the yard.

"But you have no evidence of that, either?"

Polly jumped down and chased after Bella.

"No, not yet. But I could get some." Maddie stood up. "Yesterday, I came very close to seeing what's inside one of the crates that he's been transporting on his boat. If I can prove that it's something illegal, that might give Jake a chance to question and maybe arrest him. All I need to do is watch his boat and wait for a good time to take a look."

"A stakeout!" Tammy stood up as well. "Oh, I am absolutely coming along. I'll grab us some cupcakes and coffee for the road."

"Tammy, I can do it by myself, really. You don't have to come." Maddie herded the dogs inside, behind Tammy.

"But I want to! Maddie, we've barely had a chance to see each other. We can catch up and talk about selling the bakery. Plus, I'll be there just in case you need some backup. Please?" Tammy batted her eyes and smiled.

"All right, fine. Hopefully, you'll be less distracting than these two were."

"I promise, I won't be the least bit distracting." Tammy winked.

"Okay, I just need two seconds. I just want to tell Dean we're going out." Maddie started up the stairs to his room. After a quick knock on the door, she turned the knob. The door swung open and revealed an empty room. "Dean?" Her heart skipped a beat. Had he run away? That certainly wouldn't look good. "Dean?" Her voice raised.

"Mom?" Dean stepped out of the bathroom into the hallway.

"Oh, there you are." Maddie felt a wave of relief. "Aunt Tammy and I are going to be out for a bit. I just wanted to make sure that you'd be okay."

"Yes, I'll be fine. I'm just going to call Stella." Dean walked back toward his room.

"Okay. Send her my love."

"I will." Dean closed the door behind him, and Maddie walked back down the stairs.

"All set." Tammy grabbed the two travel mugs and a container of cupcakes.

"Great, let's go see what we can find."

As Maddie settled back into the driver's seat, she glanced over at her sister.

"I'm not so sure about getting you into the middle of this."

"I'm already in the middle of it. I love Dean, too, you know." Tammy buckled her seat belt. "I'm not going anywhere."

"All right. I just hope we turn up something." Maddie started the car and backed out of the driveway. Her mind flashed back to the moment the dogs had barked the night that Ricardo was murdered. Was there something she had missed?

"You're quiet. What are you thinking?" Tammy looked over at her.

"I just feel like if I had paid closer attention when the dogs were barking near Ricardo's body, I'd know who the murderer is. I was there, and not long after he was killed."

"What could you have noticed that the police didn't?" Tammy asked. "They did a thorough search and didn't find anything that would tell them who the murderer is. I don't think much could have changed from the time that you were near the crime scene until they searched the crime scene."

"That's true. But I still wonder." Maddie turned into the parking lot of the marina. She rolled along the parking spaces and chose one near Captain Niles' boat.

*a* s Maddie parked, she peered through the windshield. "I'm not sure if Sam's there or not. But the van I saw him unloading crates from is there." She glanced around the marina. "It's too busy right now for me to get a look inside, but maybe as it gets darker, I'll get a chance."

"Great, that gives us plenty of time to chat." Tammy handed her one of the travel mugs. "And eat." She passed her a cupcake.

"This reminds me of the long drives we would take with Mom and Dad, to Great-Aunt Shirley's house in the mountains. Do you remember?" Maddie licked some frosting off her finger. "We'd camp out in the back seat and snack the whole time."

"I remember." Tammy grinned. "We used to drive them crazy with that song we would sing!"

"Oh, yes!" Maddie laughed. "I had forgotten about that song." She took a bite of her cupcake, then sat back against the seat. "I can't believe I was so out of touch with what Mom wanted. I really wish I had known how much she disliked that job she took."

"She made it work, I think. As much as she missed the bakery, she never would have been able to work in it without Dad being there."

"We were all so shocked when he died." Maddie cleared her throat.

"It came out of nowhere."

"There he is!" Maddie scooted forward in her seat as she spotted Captain Sam Niles headed for his boat. Before he could reach it, a man stepped toward him. "Isn't that Lawson?"

"I think so." Tammy and Maddie watched as Sam and Lawson had a brief conversation. Although they couldn't hear their words, from Sam's body language, he seemed to be upset. His arms were waving around, and Lawson patted the air with his hands, palms down, as if he was trying to calm him down. Sam handed over an envelope, then Lawson turned around and walked off.

"I wonder what that was about." Maddie glanced at her sister.

"Maybe something about the boat tour," Tammy suggested.

"Maybe. I want to see what Sam has to say about the murder. I want to know what he has in those crates." Maddie started to open the car door.

"If Veronica wouldn't talk to you, what makes you think that Sam will?" Tammy asked. "You might just tip him off."

"You're right, he probably won't talk to me. But he's my best lead at the moment." Maddie peered through the windshield. "I want to know exactly what he's moving on that boat. He's gone inside now. It's almost dark. I bet he won't be back out for a while." She reached for the door handle. "I'm going to see if I can get a closer look."

"Maddie, no." Tammy grabbed her arm. "What if he sees you? There's all kinds of lighting along the marina now."

"I'll be careful." Maddie pushed the door open.

"Maddie!" Tammy tugged her back inside. "It's not like you have any real experience being a detective, or a ninja! Why are you putting yourself at risk like this?"

"I'll be fine. I have to do this. It's for Dean,

Tammy." Maddie looked back at the boat as it rocked in the water. "I can't risk him ending up in prison for something he didn't do."

"All right." Tammy squeezed her arm. "But if you're going out there, so am I!"

"Tammy, you can't."

"Try and stop me!" Tammy pushed her own door open, then stepped out.

Maddie groaned with frustration. "Fine, but you have to be quiet. Just follow me and stay out of the light."

Maddie started toward Sam's boat just as he emerged from the cabin.

"Hide!" Maddie grabbed Tammy's arm and pulled her behind a large pillar.

Sam walked to the railing of the boat and looked out over it, toward the parking lot. His gaze swung right toward the pillar that Maddie and Tammy hid behind.

Maddie held her breath. She didn't dare to poke her head out to see if Sam had spotted them. After a few minutes slid by, she looked over at Tammy.

"I don't think he saw us. I'm going to take a look."

Tammy gave a short nod, her lips pressed tightly together.

Maddie peeked around the edge of the pillar and saw no sign of Sam on his boat. She scanned the marina. "He's gone. No one is around." She turned toward Tammy. "You stay here and watch for him. Warn me, if you see him. I'm going to see if I can get inside that van."

"Wouldn't it be better for me to go with you?" Tammy looked around the side of the pillar.

"It'll be much harder for him to notice anything amiss, if it's just me. Please, Tammy, you said you would help me, and this is the help that I need." Maddie held her gaze. "Just stay here and be my lookout, okay?"

"Okay." Tammy grabbed Maddie's hand. "But be careful."

"I will be." Maddie squeezed her sister's hand, then stepped out from behind the pillar. She made her way casually toward the van and attempted to stay out of the line of sight of the boat. As she reached the back doors of the van, she felt a prickle of anxiety crawl up her spine. The moment she opened the doors, she would be doing something illegal. If Sam caught her, he could call the police, or worse. She glanced around once more, then opened the back of the van.

A light turned on and revealed several large

crates, pushed back toward the front of the van. She pointed her phone's flashlight in the direction of the crates and strained to see inside of them. Unable to see anything clearly, she realized she'd have to climb inside to get a better look.

Just as she was about to crawl into the van, she heard a door slam in the parking lot.

Her heart raced as she quickly stepped back and closed the doors to the van. Had she been spotted?

As the doors closed, she heard a sharp whistle from behind her. Could it be Tammy warning her? Before she had a chance to look, a strong voice startled her.

"Who's out there?" Sam's booming voice reached her ears.

Maddie jumped as she wondered who she had heard behind her, as Sam was still on the boat.

"What's going on?" a voice called out from behind Maddie. She recognized the voice. Had Jake just caught her breaking into the van?

She quickly realized that if she'd been caught breaking into Sam's van, Jake had every reason to arrest her.

Sam stormed over to the van, his expression contorted with anger.

"What's going on here? What are you doing?" he snapped at Maddie.

"I was just out for a stroll. That's all." Maddie's heart pounded as she looked between the two men.

"A stroll that led you straight toward my van? I think you need to watch where you're walking." Sam glared at her. "I think I saw you close the door on the van. Did you break into it?"

"She was just walking past, no harm done." Jake's voice hardened as he shifted closer to Maddie. "Unless you want me to take a look in the van with you to make sure."

"Gee, thanks for the offer." Sam rolled his eyes, then stalked back toward his boat.

"Come with me." Jake's voice had an air of authority to it. "We need to talk away from prying ears." He led her toward his car. When they reached it, he turned to look at her. "What were you doing?"

"Nothing." Maddie's heart pounded. "Like I said, I was just going for a walk."

"A walk?" Jake asked incredulously. "A walk right by Sam's boat? A walk right to Sam's van?"

"It was a coincidence."

"I don't believe that for a second." Jake shook his head. "You need to be careful, Maddie."

"I'll be fine." Maddie crossed her arms.

"You always say that." Jake sighed. "You've always said that."

"And I will be." Maddie met his eyes.

"Okay, if you say so." Jake held up his hands and took a step back toward his car. "If you'd rather be stubborn than safe, then go ahead. You've always made that choice." He got into the front seat and closed the door. The engine roared to life.

Maddie watched him drive away as she started toward her own car. The headlights of Jake's car brightened, illuminating her path as he drove away.

Maddie rolled her eyes and sighed. Jake had always been impossible to shake off. It seemed that quality hadn't faded with age. She quickened her pace. The sound of a car horn disrupted her thoughts. Maddie jumped as she looked into the headlights of a car coming toward her. She was relieved to see that it was her own car.

Tammy rolled down the window and stuck her head out.

"I'm so sorry, Maddie. I tried to warn you. I whistled, but I was too late. I guess I'm not a great lookout." She scanned the parking lot. "I just saw Jake leave. I thought he was going to take you to the police station. I thought he might even arrest you."

"No, he just warned me to be careful." Maddie climbed into the passenger seat.

"He's always looking out for you." Tammy smiled as she pulled away from the curb.

"I don't know why." Maddie laughed.

"You seem to have a place in his heart." Tammy turned in the direction of the house.

Maddie thought over Tammy's words. Maybe Tammy was right. Ever since they were in school, he was always looking out for her.

# CHAPTER 22

*T*ammy pulled into Maddie's driveway, and Maddie followed her up the porch steps.

Tammy opened the front door and froze.

"Dean? What are you doing with your bag?"

Dean stood in the doorway with his bag in one hand and his phone in the other.

"Don't try to stop me, Aunt Tammy."

Maddie pushed past Tammy and stared into her son's eyes. "What are you doing?" She stepped in front of him before he could get through the door.

"Mom, I have to go." Dean shied back from her. "I know, it's not what you want, but I have no choice. They found my sunglasses by his body, Mom! They're going to arrest me. I know it!"

"I know you want to run away, Dean. You have reason to want to. But I need you to listen to me. If you go now, it's going to be so much harder to clear your name." Maddie grabbed his hand and squeezed it. "I'm getting closer to the truth. I promise. I'm not going to let anything happen to you."

"Mom." Dean pulled his hand away from her. "I know that you think you can always protect me. But you can't. You can't stop the police from arresting me. You can't stop a jury from convicting me. This is my last chance to get away. I'm not asking you to help me. I'm just asking you not to stop me."

As Dean's bright blue eyes, the same shade as her own, looked into hers, she felt a familiar tug of urgency. From the day he was born she'd felt a primal desire to protect him. It hadn't faded with time.

"Dean, this isn't the way." Maddie insisted. "I'm going to keep you safe. I promise you that. But if you run, it's only going to make things harder. If I believed this was the best way to protect you, I would be ushering you out the door right this second."

"You're falling for his scam, aren't you, Mom?" Dean narrowed his eyes. "I don't know what kind of power that man has over you, but you are being blinded by him. He's not going to help us. He's not going to help me."

"I'm not falling for anything, Dean." Maddie turned him back toward the living room. "I'm asking you to give me a little more time. If things don't seem to be panning out in a good way, then I'll smuggle you onto the next flight out of town. All right?"

"Okay." Dean ran his hands across his face. "One day. I'll give it one more day. All right?" He lowered his hands and looked into her eyes. "I don't want to be locked away."

"I'm not going to let that happen. I promise." Maddie took his hands and squeezed them. "But you're going to have to help me. What happened to your sunglasses?"

"I have no idea. All I can think is that they must have fallen out of my pocket somewhere around town, and maybe Ricardo picked them up? Or maybe he somehow got them off me when I spoke to him. But I didn't see him pick them up before he walked off." Dean tried to remember all the details of their encounter. "I feel like an idiot for not knowing that they were gone, but I just didn't notice. I know that Jake doesn't believe me. But you have to, Mom. I'm telling the truth."

"I know you are." Maddie met his eyes. "Can you remember the last time you knew for sure that you were wearing them? The last time you had them?"

"At the restaurant. When I first arrived. I remember taking them off and putting them on the table when I sat down, when I was waiting for you. I've been meaning to get a new pair but haven't gotten round to it. One of the arms was very loose. So, they won't sit on my head." Dean ran his hand through his hair. "But after that, I just have no idea."

"That's all right. That's a good start. I can ask Janet if she noticed anyone pick up a pair of sunglasses. Maybe someone found them and sold them to Ricardo." Maddie sat down on the couch next to him. "We'll get it all figured out."

"I don't think anyone would have sold them, Mom. They weren't worth much. I can't see anyone paying anything for them. They're just old sunglasses that Dad bought for me when I graduated from high school. I had wanted them so bad and he bought them for me. They weren't worth much then, and they're worth even less now."

"I remember that." Maddie smiled as the memory filled her mind. "You loved the fact that

CINDY BELL

Dad had given you something that you really wanted."

"I've been meaning to replace them." Dean scowled.

"Dean." Maddie rubbed his arm. "You don't have to hate your father. You know that, don't you? He made some mistakes, but he's still the same man that went to your graduation, with tears in his eyes. He's still so incredibly proud of you."

"I don't want to talk about it, Mom." Dean stood up from the couch. "I'll be in my room."

Maddie watched as Dean walked toward the stairs. As angry as she was at Craig when she'd first found out about all the lies, it had never crossed her mind that he wasn't a good father. She stepped back out onto the porch and forced all thoughts of her ex-husband from her mind. She needed to find out how Ricardo ended up with Dean's sunglasses, and fast.

As Maddie closed the door behind her, she took a deep breath. She'd just promised her son that she would keep him out of prison. She needed to do everything she could to keep that promise. Would there still be time for him to run if things didn't go the way that she hoped?

"You have to make sure you get to the truth," Maddie muttered. "It's time to work this all out."

She'd start with the restaurant, then she'd move on to Sam's boat. As her gaze swept toward the driveway, her breath caught in her throat. A large man, with bushy eyebrows, and a menacing glare, stepped up onto the porch. It only took her a moment to recognize him as the same man that had argued with Sam when they disembarked after the boat tour. Iris said his name was Alex. Instinctively, Maddie took a step back toward the door.

"Don't run off, love." A smile spread across Alex's lips as he met her eyes. "I just want to talk."

# CHAPTER 23

"Who are you?" Maddie did her best to pretend that she didn't recognize him.

"That doesn't really matter." Alex rubbed the stubble along his chin. "I'm here to help you out. I'm a friend."

"If someone is my friend, I usually know their name." Maddie stood her ground but wondered how dangerous he might be. "What are you doing here?"

"I saw you snooping around Sam's van." Alex lowered his voice. "Do you want to know what he's up to or not?" He leaned against the post and looked into her eyes. "I can tell you more than your cop friend, that's for sure."

"I don't have a cop friend." Maddie crossed her arms.

"Oh, I'm sorry. I meant, the chief of police." Alex smirked. "He thinks he knows everything, but he doesn't have a clue. So much goes on in this town that he never notices."

"What do you know?" Maddie walked to the edge of the porch and looked straight at him. "Tell me!"

"Tell you? Is that supposed to intimidate me?" Alex chuckled. "Sorry, but that's not going to work on me."

"What do you want?" Maddie took a slight step back as he leaned closer to her. "Money?"

"I want you to make sure that your cop friend looks in a new direction. It's bad enough that Ricardo was killed, but now I have the cops breathing down my neck. It's really bad for my business." Alex shrugged. "I didn't kill Ricardo, but the longer they're on my back about it, the harder it is for me to operate. So, I'll give you the information, in exchange for your assurance that you'll give it to the police without mentioning where you got it, and I can have the attention off me and continue to conduct my business in peace."

"I can't do that." Maddie's curiosity launched

into hyperdrive. What information could he possibly have? "For all I know you could be the murderer."

"I'm not. Why would I kill someone who hired me? I have to pay my bills. I'm not a murderer. But I hear your son might be." Alex looked toward the house. "Is he in there?" He smiled as he looked back at her. "I'm the one that called in the tip about his argument with Ricardo. Maybe I should call in another tip about how those sunglasses ended up next to Ricardo's body? Maybe I saw more than I admitted? I can tell you right now, if I get hauled into that police station, I can spin a great story for them that will put your little Dean right in the spotlight."

"No, don't do that." The false sense of power Maddie had felt since the moment he asked to talk deflated. "Dean had nothing to do with Ricardo's murder!"

"Sure, he's innocent. Just like I am. But the cold hard justice system doesn't care about the truth, does it? It just wants a closed case, and someone doing time. So, either you can help me make sure that there's a better suspect, or you can stand back and watch me hang your kid out to dry. What's it going to be?" Alex tipped his head to the side as he lowered his voice. "We'll be doing each other a favor, really."

"How do I know you're not Ricardo's murderer? You could have gotten angry with him. Maybe you wanted to take over his business. I'm not going to help you get away with murder." Maddie tried to infuse her voice with confidence.

"I wasn't anywhere near Ricardo when he was killed. I was doing what he told me to do, hunting down Tim. He wasn't returning Ricardo's calls, and he was mad. He told me to find Tim and take whatever he had on him. I didn't kill Ricardo, and Tim can vouch for that." Alex looked into her eyes. "So, what do you say?"

"I say that you're a liar." Maddie glared at him. "I know that Tim called Ricardo about twenty minutes before he was killed. Which means he wasn't avoiding Ricardo's calls, and you're lying about what you were doing."

"I'm not lying." Alex scowled. "There's no way Tim called Ricardo. I was with him on the other side of town. He didn't even have his phone on him. I searched his pockets for every single thing he had on him to take back to Ricardo. There wasn't a phone."

"That's impossible."

"As impossible as your son being arrested for murder? Because that's what's about to happen." Alex turned toward the steps. "You had your chance."

"Wait!" Maddie neared the edge of the porch. "What information do you have?"

Alex turned back toward her. She searched his expression for any hint of his intentions.

A smile lingered on his lips.

"It's about Sam Niles, and his illegal activities. I can give you evidence that he's been smuggling guns and stolen goods, and that Ricardo wanted in on it. But before I do any of that, you have to promise me you're going to give this information to the police and push the investigation in Sam's direction. I'll give you the address of his warehouse to start. That should give the police enough to arrest Sam and leave me alone. Once that's done, and I know you kept your end of the bargain, I'll send through the rest of the details. What do you say?" He held his hand out to her. "Are we a team?"

Maddie's skin crawled at the thought of taking his hand. If circumstances had been different, she guessed that he would have been threatening her after he finished with Sam. But with Ricardo dead, she hoped that maybe Craig's debt had died with him.

"I'll give them the information." Maddie took his hand and shook it.

"Brilliant." Alex clenched his jaw. "Don't let me down."

"I won't."

"Make sure you don't." Alex released her hand.

"But after this, you have nothing to do with me or my family."

"Is that how you think it works? Your husband still owes money, doesn't he?" Alex tilted his head to the side as he smiled at her. "Maybe, if you do a really good job, I'll do you another favor and get rid of that thorn in your side. I have some connections behind bars. They owe me some favors."

"No, don't do that." Maddie's heart pounded. "Please!"

"Look at you." Alex laughed as he started to descend the steps of the front porch. "After everything he's done to you, you still want to protect him?" He peered up at her from the front walkway. "They don't make women like you anymore, you know." He brushed his hand back through his thick hair. "Don't worry, I told you already, I'm not a murderer, remember?"

Maddie stared after him as he trotted down the walkway and out through the front gate. She immediately felt her muscles relax as he walked away.

A few seconds later, Maddie's phone buzzed with the text he'd sent. She looked down at the message and read the address of the warehouse. If she gave the information to Jake, and directed his attention toward Sam, she'd be potentially shielding Alex. It was still possible he was a murderer. The best way to try and work out if Alex was innocent, was to find out if he was telling the truth. She noticed a dark blue sedan drive past her house. Had Alex been the one following her? She imagined he must have been.

She took a deep breath and headed to her car, but instead of driving toward the restaurant, she headed straight back to Tim's house.

# CHAPTER 24

*M*addie knocked on Tim's front door at the same moment that Jake's patrol car rolled to a stop behind her SUV in the driveway.

"What are you doing here?" Jake stepped out of the car and strode toward Maddie just as the front door swung open.

"Can I help you?" Tim stood in the doorway, his eyes narrowed as he looked at them. "I was just on my way out."

"I need to speak to you, Tim?" Jake's muscles tensed as he reached the door and tried to peer past Tim into the house. "Is Veronica here?"

"Is this about yesterday?" Tim glared at Maddie. "We just had a disagreement."

"No, it's not about that." Jake drew his attention back to him. "I would like to speak to her."

"No, she's not here." Tim shook his head.

Maddie doubted that Jake wanted her listening to their conversation, but she wanted to hear what they were saying, so she decided to stand there until he objected.

"I need to know why you called Ricardo shortly before he was killed." Jake concentrated on Tim.

"I didn't." Tim scrunched up his nose.

"Call records show you did, so don't bother lying to me." Jake narrowed his eyes. "What was your business with Ricardo?"

"I already told you, I didn't have any business with him." Tim took a step through the doorway. "Are you here to arrest me? Because, if not, I have places to be. Not everything in this town comes to a grinding halt when someone dies."

"Wait just a second." Jake stood his ground and blocked Tim's path. "How do you explain a call placed from your phone at that time?"

"I don't know about any call," Tim huffed as he looked away from him. "I lost my phone. Okay? I've been looking for it, but I haven't been able to find it. I just got a new one." He pulled a phone out of his pocket. "See?"

"Can you tell me where you were, then?" Jake didn't move away from him. "At home, sleeping?"

"No." Tim crossed his arms over his chest. "I was out. I couldn't sleep."

"Where were you?" Jake took a step toward him. "Were you alone?"

Tim stared at him for a moment, then sighed.

"No, I wasn't alone."

"Who were you with?" Jake met Tim's eyes. "Another woman?"

"No! It wasn't like that." Tim scowled. "I was out walking, and this guy started roughing me up. Basically mugged me. He searched my pockets, but I didn't have anything. So, he let me go."

"Without getting the money for Ricardo?" Maddie crossed her arms as she ignored Jake's warning glance at her.

A startled expression crossed Tim's face as he stared at her.

"You were with Alex, weren't you?" Maddie locked her eyes to his. "Because you'd been dodging Ricardo's calls and demands for payment. Is that why you lost your phone? So, Ricardo would leave you alone?"

"No! I just lost it. I had it one minute, and the next I couldn't find it anywhere. Okay?" Tim pushed past both of them. "I don't have anything else to say."

"I thought you didn't have any business with Ricardo?" Jake followed after him.

"I don't now, do I?" Tim glared at Jake. "Are you going to arrest me or not? I wasn't alone, and I didn't make that call. I lost my phone a couple of days ago. I didn't have anything to do with Ricardo being killed!"

"Okay. You're free to go. At least for the moment." Jake watched him as he settled into his car. He stepped up beside Maddie, as Tim backed his car down the driveway. "What was that, Maddie? How did you know about Alex?"

"Alex told me he was with Tim, and that Tim didn't have a phone on him. Just like Tim just said. That means he's not lying about not making the call. It means that neither of them killed Ricardo. But someone had Tim's phone." Maddie glanced over at Jake and noticed the scrutiny in his gaze.

"I don't know how much faith we can put in the word of a loan shark's enforcer." Jake quirked an eyebrow. "When did Alex tell you this? He could be lying. They both could be."

"Maybe you're right." Maddie gazed into space for a moment as she imagined the scenario playing out. She looked back at him. "But it doesn't make sense, does it? Alex and Tim's stories match up. They both claim they were together at the time. Even if Tim did have his phone with him, why would he call Ricardo when Alex threatened him? Why would he want to risk being hurt or even killed by getting Ricardo's attention?"

"Maybe he wanted to make a deal with him? I've seen it before. People can get pretty desperate when men like Alex threaten them. Maybe, he decided to reach out to Ricardo in an attempt to settle things up."

"It's possible. Can you tell where the cell phone was when the call to Ricardo was made?" Maddie asked.

Jake tipped his head toward his car.

"Meet me back at the station. We'll go over it." He looked straight into her eyes. "All of it. I feel like you have more to tell me."

Again, he spoke to her with a sense of familiarity, which surprised her. She watched as he returned to his car.

Jake glanced back at her as he opened the door.

"Are you going to meet me there?"

"Yes." Maddie climbed into her SUV. As she drove to the station, she thought about what Tim had said. He'd lost his phone. It had been there one minute and gone the next. What were the chances that someone just happened upon his phone and called Ricardo? She inhaled sharply as she suddenly realized what his missing phone might mean. Someone had stolen it, and whoever stole it, likely killed Ricardo.

# CHAPTER 25

*M*addie pulled into the police station and parked in the first spot she saw. She hurried toward the front doors in search of Jake. She caught sight of him as he turned down a hallway and stepped into his office.

She followed after him, with only a brief look of curiosity from Noreen.

"Let me see." Jake picked up a file on his desk and paged through it. "The call was made from Tim's address."

"So, maybe Tim and Alex really are lying." Maddie glanced over her shoulder at the people milling about the police station, then stepped into his office and closed the door.

"It looks like it." Jake read over the papers. "Unless someone else used his phone at his house."

"I do have some information for you."

"I'm all ears." Jake leaned back in his office chair.

"Sam Niles is running a smuggling ring." Maddie sat down in the chair in front of his desk. "I can give you the address of the warehouse where he's storing the goods he's transporting."

"What goods?" Jake sat forward and looked straight into her eyes.

"Apparently, guns and stolen items. I don't know more than that." Maddie frowned. "I do know that it's illegal, and Ricardo wanted in. That's all the information I have."

"Who did you get the information from?" Jake picked a pen up from his desk and began jotting notes down on a pad beside his keyboard.

"I can't tell you." Maddie watched as he looked up at her.

"Of course you can tell me. This information is meaningless without a worthwhile source." Jake set the pen down. "Who gave you the information?"

"Okay, I'll handle it myself." Maddie stood up and turned toward the door.

"Maddie, why can't you just tell me what I need

to know?" Jake stood up and walked around the side of his desk. "I need to be able to trace it back. Without knowing its original source, I won't have a trail to follow. Was it Alex?" Jake leaned back against the front of his desk. "I mean, you knew about him and Tim being together, so was it Alex?"

"I can't say." Maddie took a step back. "If you don't want the address, I'll go check the warehouse out myself."

"I'll take it."

"If you can find out who took Tim's phone, I bet you can figure out who actually killed Ricardo," Maddie suggested. "I'm pretty convinced it was Sam Niles, but I don't know why he would have taken Tim's phone."

"Maybe to make it look like Tim had called Ricardo, to throw off the investigation?" Jake rubbed his hands together as he looked up at the ceiling. "This is just a theory, but maybe Tim found out about the smuggling. Maybe he threatened to go to the police, so Sam needed to get rid of him. He killed Ricardo, and made it look like Tim did it."

"I don't know." Maddie sighed. "That's a lot of work just to make Tim look guilty. And how would any of that explain Dean's sunglasses ending up beside Ricardo's body? None of it adds up, right?"

"Right."

"If Sam is smuggling guns or something else, and Ricardo wanted to be involved, that means Sam might have had a reason to want to get rid of Ricardo. If I can get the evidence from the warehouse, then you can arrest him, right? At least for the smuggling."

"No, you're not going anywhere near that warehouse. I'll take care of it. I'll make sure that we find the evidence, and that Sam is arrested, if he's guilty." Jake stood up from where he'd been leaning against his desk. "Just give me the address, and I'll get right on it."

"I'll text it to you." Maddie reached for the door.

"Maddie, just leave this to me." Jake walked closer to her. "If Sam is the murderer, he's dangerous."

"I know." Maddie stepped through the door. She'd almost made it to her car when she spotted Veronica stepping out of hers. The sight of Tim's wife sparked a series of connections in her mind.

"Veronica!" Maddie rushed toward her. "I need to speak to you!"

# CHAPTER 26

*V*eronica froze, then turned slowly to look at Maddie. "About what?"

"It was you, wasn't it?" Maddie stopped a few feet from her. "You're the one who called Ricardo."

"I don't know what you're talking about." Veronica crossed her arms.

"Is that what you and Tim were arguing about at the marina? Did he find out what you did?" Maddie stared hard into her eyes. "Or did he already know?"

"Okay, fine, yes, you caught me." Veronica rolled her eyes and exhaled loudly. "I made the call to Ricardo."

"But why?" Maddie moved closer to her. "Did you ask him to meet with you?"

"Yes, I did. I had to." Veronica crossed her arms. "Ricardo was harassing Tim. He wouldn't leave him alone. I could tell he was scared, and my husband never gets scared. So, I figured I would handle things." She shrugged. "I took Tim's phone so Ricardo couldn't contact him while all of this was happening. I didn't want Tim to get in the middle of it and get hurt. I called Ricardo from Tim's phone and set up the meeting, so I could talk to him about giving back the money I'd borrowed from him."

"The money you borrowed from him?" Maddie's eyes widened. "Are you saying it wasn't Tim that took money from Ricardo?"

"No. It wasn't. Tim likes to do everything by the book. But we were drowning. In order to have the high-end business partners that Tim has, he has to look the part. Our house has to look the part. I have to look the part. Our funds were running dry, because that stupid amusement park took forever to get approved. It's taking forever to start building, and costs keep going up. Everyone's putting pressure on him. So, I did what I had to do to make sure that Tim had what he needed. I was desperate. We needed the money. Lawson mentioned to me that Ricardo had helped him out when he started his business, and he might be able to help us out. So, I went to Ricardo." Veronica cleared her throat. "Really, it was the only thing I could do."

"It wasn't." Maddie realized that it was likely that her ex-husband felt the same way. He probably thought going to Ricardo for money was his only option. "You could have talked to Tim. You could have done anything other than put yourself and your husband in that kind of danger."

"I know that now." Veronica sighed as she looked toward the police station. "Which is why I'm here. With the way the police are investigating Tim, I need to tell the truth. I can't have Tim go to jail for something that he didn't do." She looked back at Maddie.

"What did Ricardo say when you met with him?" Maddie's heartbeat quickened. "Was there anyone else there with him?"

"I was never going to go myself." Veronica rolled her eyes. "I'm not that stupid. I sent someone else to speak to him."

"Someone else? Who?"

"My gardener, Chip. I offered to pay him a little extra, if he would handle the situation for me. Honestly, I thought Ricardo might be intimidated by him." Veronica bit into her bottom lip. "I never thought things would get out of hand."

"Out of hand? Did he kill Ricardo?" Relief rushed through Maddie at the thought of the murder being solved. "Where is he now?"

"I have no idea. He took off. He said that he didn't do it. He claimed that when he went there to meet him, he heard dogs barking and then saw police lights. He figured that Ricardo had either been arrested, or was scared off by the cops, so he left. But of course, that's just the story he's telling." Veronica winced. "It solved my problem, so I wasn't going to turn him in, but now that the police are after Tim, I have to tell the police."

"You're doing the right thing." Maddie sighed with relief. "Finally, all of this can be over. Do you want me to walk in with you?"

"No, it's all right. I can handle this." Veronica straightened her shoulders and looked toward the police station. "I just hope that they don't think I was involved in the murder. I wasn't. I just made a stupid decision. When I told Tim about borrowing the money, he was furious. That's why we were arguing at the marina. He was so angry about what I'd done. Getting involved with Ricardo. But he had no idea I used his phone and set up the meeting. He will soon know everything, of course, and I'll have to deal with it. But at least the police will be off his back." She met Maddie's eyes. "He's not the easiest man, but he really does love me. I just wish I hadn't caused him so much trouble." She walked toward the door of the police station.

Maddie stared after her. A part of her wondered if she did hire Chip to kill Ricardo, and now wanted to make up a story to cover it up. Maybe what Chip had said was exactly what happened. She recalled the way the dogs had barked at him at Veronica's house. They had barked the same way just before Ricardo's body had been found. Did that mean that Chip was telling the truth about not arriving until after Ricardo had already been killed? Did that mean that Chip hadn't killed Ricardo?

Maddie wanted to get right back in her car, go home, and celebrate with her son that a murderer had been caught. She imagined that there would be plenty of evidence to arrest Chip, with Veronica's testimony. But what if he was telling the truth?

Maddie tried to remember exactly how the night unfolded. The dogs began barking and pulling before they reached the fence. When the police had reached Ricardo, he had been dead for a little while. If Chip had killed him, why would he hang around and wait for the police to arrive?

What if the police decided Chip didn't do it?

What if they turned their attention right back on Dean? She needed to make sure that the murderer was behind bars. Instead of turning back to her car, she started down the sidewalk in the direction of Janet's Place. She still wanted to find out who took Dean's sunglasses, and how Ricardo ended up with them.

As Maddie walked, her mind flooded with what she had learned. She imagined that Jake would hear Veronica's story, and rush right out to arrest Chip. But what if he wasn't the murderer?

Suddenly, she felt a hard push against her back. Startled, she stumbled forward. Before she had a chance to regain her balance, a hood came down over her head, blinding her to her surroundings. She opened her mouth to scream, but a hand clamped down over it before she could. Strong arms wrapped around her own, pinning them to her sides.

# CHAPTER 27

$\mathcal{M}$addie attempted to squirm out of her assailant's grasp. Panic flooded through her as he easily wrestled her in the direction he chose. Her mind grew fuzzy with fear and a certainty that she couldn't breathe through the palm plastered across her mouth. The world around her shifted as he pulled her forward.

"Not a word, got it?"

Maddie's heart dropped. She recognized his voice. Lawson. She felt the metal ramp that her shoes struck as he continued to drag her away from the parking lot. He was dragging her through the marina. She tried to fight against him, but he only tightened his grip. Within just a few short minutes, her hands were tied, along with her feet. The hood remained over her head.

"Please, just tell me why you're doing this!" Maddie's voice trembled. "Lawson, how do you have anything to do with this? Why are you doing this?"

"You gave me no other choice," Lawson growled. "You were going to ruin the good little smuggling business I have going."

"You and Sam were in on this together?" Maddie gasped.

"Not the murder, no. That was all me." Lawson's voice became edged with pride. "I set up the smuggling business, Sam just had to drive a boat. How hard is that? I lent him the money to buy his boat and start the boat tours. When Ricardo found out what we were up to with the smuggling, he wanted in. He wanted a cut of the profits. When I refused, he sent his goon after me. I borrowed money from Ricardo a long time ago, and I paid off my debts. I owed him nothing. And now, all of a sudden, he was trying to get in on our business. I couldn't let that happen, so I took care of Alex by paying him off, and I took care of Ricardo by getting rid of him. When Alex came after us, Sam got cold feet, said he was going to shut everything down."

"So, Sam wanted out?" Maddie tried to slow her racing heart.

"Yes, I said if he didn't want to do it anymore, I would get another captain, another boat. Sam said he couldn't live in fear. He was going to meet with Ricardo that night. He was going to tell him he wanted nothing to do with any of it. He called him and set up the meeting. I convinced him not to go. I said I would deal with things. So, I went instead. Things got out of hand. I couldn't let Ricardo ruin my business. I did what I had to do. I took care of things." Lawson sighed. "Sam found out what I did. He threatened to turn me in. So, I have to take care of him, too."

"You killed him?" Maddie gasped.

"No. Well, at least not yet," Lawson said slowly. "Everything was going to plan. But now you keep snooping around Sam. You keep snooping around the boat, and the crates. You brought the police's attention to the business. It won't be long before everyone is snooping around me. I can't keep smuggling the goods with the cops all over everything, so that means I have to get rid of the problem and relocate the business." He yanked the hood off Maddie's head. "And since you seem so determined to expose the smuggling ring and catch Ricardo's murderer, you're going to disappear, too."

Maddie blinked at the bright light and tried to focus. She looked around the boat. In the corner, she saw Sam lying on the floor with ropes around his legs and arms. He wasn't moving. Was he dead?

"Dean lost his sunglasses here, on the boat, didn't he?" Maddie's heart raced as she recalled their tour, and Lawson boarding the boat after them. "Or did you somehow steal them from him?"

"He must have dropped them on the boat. I found them, and Sam mentioned that he thought they were Dean's. I kept them. I figured finders keepers, but then I found out Ricardo was trying to collect from Dean, too, so I decided to try to pin his murder on him. It would have worked out just fine, if you hadn't gotten involved." Lawson glared at her.

"You don't have to do this." Maddie's voice wavered.

"Oh, but I do." Lawson smirked. "I'm going to sink this boat with you and Sam on it. I already have another captain to take over the transportation side of the business. The warehouse has already been cleared out. The goods have been relocated. I've taken care of everything, so the police won't find any real evidence that anything illegal is going on. Any investigations will go down with Sam and his boat. Oh, and you. I'll keep the business running, away from prying eyes. It's a perfect plan."

Tears filled Maddie's eyes as she heard the coldness in his voice.

As she was about to fight for her life, the cabin door burst open. Jake stormed inside with his gun pointed at Lawson.

"On your knees! Hands behind your head!" His powerful voice echoed throughout the small space.

Lawson dropped to his knees and raised his hands in the air.

Jake rushed forward and grabbed Lawson hard by the shoulder. His gaze burned into Maddie's. "Did he hurt you?" His voice was tinged with fury.

"No." Maddie watched Jake handcuff Lawson. "No, he didn't hurt me."

Maddie noticed Sam squirm. It looked like he was going to be okay.

An officer walked over to Sam as Jake yanked Lawson to his feet.

"I guess the murderer has been caught." Jake met Maddie's eyes. "You sit tight. Someone will be right in to untie you and make sure that you get checked out."

# CHAPTER 28

The next afternoon, after seeing Dean off and baking cupcakes with Tammy, Maddie began to feel the shock of what had occurred wear off. She'd been so stunned to see Jake charge to her rescue. It still baffled her how he always seemed to know when she was in trouble.

Now, Maddie stood outside the bakery beside a table of cupcakes. Tammy had insisted they bake them and have them at the front for the locals before the place was sold. As a send-off to the bakery. The whole thing felt bittersweet to Maddie.

"So, this is it?" Maddie looked at the bakery. "We're actually selling the place."

"Well, there are a few things I need to tell you."

Tammy placed another silver tray filled with cupcakes on the table.

"You do?"

"Brad got a transfer. He's been wanting this new position for ages, but it only just came through." Tammy clapped her hands.

"That's fantastic." Maddie smiled. "Tell him congratulations."

"That's not the best part." Tammy met her sister's eyes. "It's in Harborview."

"Oh, wow!" Maddie gasped. "That's only a couple of towns away."

"It's better than that." Tammy's voice raised with excitement. "We're going to move to Bayview."

"What?" Maddie's mouth fell open. "Bayview?"

"Yes, Brad's work has already organized a place." Tammy looked into her eyes. "Won't it be fun, Maddie. It's been so long since we lived close to each other, and I've missed you."

"I've missed you, too."

"Being back here has brought up so many good memories for me. It feels more like home than any home I have ever lived in. I guess, I just didn't realize how much I missed it, until I came to visit." Tammy grabbed her sister's hand. "I was going to talk to you about it when I first found out, but you've been so caught up with everything, and I wanted to make sure it was all going to work out."

"You kept it from me?"

"I don't mean to horn in on your adventure. If you'd rather we didn't move to town, we can move to Harborview. I understand." Tammy started to pull her hand back.

"Any adventure I share with you is a great adventure." Maddie squeezed her hand.

"Speaking of adventures." Tammy looked over at Amber and Iris walking toward them. "Don't be mad."

"What? Why?"

"I didn't sell the bakery. I stopped the sale. I just couldn't do it," Tammy blurted out.

"You didn't?" Maddie frowned, but a sense of relief washed over her.

"Amber and I have a plan." Tammy met Amber's eyes.

"Have you been scheming behind my back again?" Maddie looked between them.

"Maybe. Be honest. Say no if you don't want to. But what do you think about running the bakery with Katie? She's got quite a bit of experience now. She says she's ready for something new. She loves the idea. I'll help of course. But what do you think?

With all the cleaning we've been doing for the sale, we can basically have the place up and running again in no time." Tammy's cheeks flushed at the thought. "Peter offered to work part-time as well. He's eager to help out. His breads are delicious."

"Well, you've certainly been busy." Maddie's mind swam with all the news.

"I just wanted to give you another chance. It would be so good to open it. But we can't do it without you." Tammy squealed with glee as she gestured to Maddie. "I mean, if you think it's a good idea, of course. Do you?"

"Maybe." When Maddie thought the bakery had been sold, a sadness had come over her. Maybe this was what she needed.

"Wouldn't it be fun to get this place going again?" Tammy asked.

"It would. And I would love to work with Katie." Maddie's heart raced at the thought. "But I still have no money."

"It's okay. We'll work it all out." Tammy waved her hand through the air.

"We sort of applied for the grant. We had to go ahead with it because they were being snapped up so fast. They're trying to give the chance to locals to open up businesses before the big corporations come in." Amber smiled. "We applied, but if you don't want to go ahead, we can just cancel the application."

"I can't wait to get it all set up! If you decide it's a yes, I mean." Tammy laughed. "Do you really think that we can get the grant, Amber?"

"We should find out soon." Amber squeezed Maddie's shoulder. "I know that it's a lot to think about, but the thought of being able to pop in and see you every morning for my coffee and a bagel, makes me so happy."

"Me, too." Maddie took a deep breath as she looked at the building. She imagined opening the bakery and being surrounded by people she enjoyed spending time with. "I would love to open it again." She felt a bolt of excitement. "I've always been so cautious about things. I've always thought that making the right thought-out choices would lead to an easy life. But being careful didn't stop Craig from doing what he did. I think I'm ready to stop being careful. I'm ready to start taking some chances. But we still need the grant."

"That's the Maddie I've been looking for!" Tammy clapped her hands and grinned. "Look out Bayview, she's back!"

"Yes, she is." Amber's phone beeped with a text.

She looked it over, and her smile grew wide. "It's approved."

Maddie's heart fluttered with excitement. She hugged her sister and Amber, then thought about her dad wanting her to take over the bakery. It's finally happening. Better late than never. She smiled to herself at the thought of what his response might be. 'Sooner would have been better, but I'll take it.'

Tammy drew Maddie's attention back to her.

"You can use this as a sort of soft opening. It's a taste of what's to come. I'll go around and let everyone know plans have changed." Tammy's voice squeaked with excitement. "We're opening up!"

"You do that." Maddie smiled as a crowd started to gather around the cupcakes. She brushed some flour from the sleeve of her blouse and rolled her eyes. "I'm a mess."

"I see someone who doesn't seem to mind." Amber nudged her with her elbow and grinned at Tammy. "Jake is heading this way."

Maddie looked over at Jake and locked eyes with him. The sight of him made her heart skip a beat. The feeling surprised her.

"I'll just be a second." Maddie walked toward him.

"Maddie." Jake removed his hat. "How are you?"

"I'm good. Thank you again for rescuing me yesterday."

"Just doing my job." Jake winked.

"How did you know that Lawson abducted me?" Maddie asked.

"I was going to speak to Chip, and I caught sight of Lawson when he grabbed you. I only wish I hadn't been so far away." Jake took a sharp breath.

"Well, lucky you were there." Maddie smiled. "You saved my life, Jake."

"I would tell you to be more careful, but we know that won't make a difference." Jake gave a short laugh. "I just wanted to wish you luck with the sale of the bakery."

"Actually, it looks like we aren't selling it." As Maddie said the words, the reality of them hit her. "We're going to open it. Katie, Tammy's daughter, is going to run it with me."

"You are? That's great." Jake looked toward the building, then back at her as he held his hand out to shake hers. "A new beginning."

Maddie stared into his eyes. She wrapped her hand around his and continued to hold his gaze. She felt her heart skip a beat as his lips spread into a smile. Never once in all the time that she'd known him growing up had she felt attracted to him, so what was that strange flutter in her stomach.

"Can I try one of those cupcakes?" Jake pulled his hand away from hers and walked over to the table.

"Maddie, come join in the fun!" Amber grabbed her hand and tugged her toward the crowd. "Everyone wants to know when the bakery will officially open."

Maddie looked up at the same bakery that she had grown up in. Yes, everything looked the same, but somehow, everything had changed. But the one thing she knew was that this was the new start she had been hoping for. Things seemed to be falling into place. Bayview felt like where she was meant to be. She couldn't wait to continue on her new adventure!

The End

# MADDIE'S RASPBERRY CUPCAKES WITH CREAM CHEESE FROSTING RECIPE

*Ingredients:*

## Cupcakes

1 1/2 cups all-purpose flour

1 teaspoon baking powder

1/4 teaspoon salt

1/2 cup (1 stick) unsalted butter, softened to room temperature

1 cup superfine sugar

2 eggs, at room temperature

1 teaspoon vanilla extract

1/2 cup buttermilk, at room temperature

1 cup raspberries, fresh or frozen

## Cream Cheese Frosting

1 (8 ounces) package brick style cream cheese, softened to room temperature

1/2 cup (1 stick) butter, softened to room temperature

1 teaspoon vanilla extract

2 1/2 cups confectioners' sugar

12 raspberries for decorating, fresh or frozen

### *Preparation:*

Preheat the oven to 350 degrees Fahrenheit. Line a 12 cup muffin pan with paper cupcake liners. This recipe makes 12 cupcakes.

Sift together the flour, baking powder, and salt into a bowl.

In another bowl, cream together the butter and sugar until light and fluffy.

Gradually add the eggs and vanilla extract.

Mix in the dry ingredients, alternating with the buttermilk.

Either divide the batter between the prepared cupcake liners, then add the raspberries so they are evenly distributed, or gently stir the raspberries into the batter, being careful not to squash them.

Divide the batter between the cupcake liners.

Bake in the pre-heated oven for about 20 to 24 minutes, until a toothpick inserted into the middle comes out clean.

Leave the cupcakes to cool in the muffin pan for about 10 minutes, then remove from the pan and cool on a wire rack.

To make the cream cheese frosting, beat the cream cheese until smooth, add the butter and beat together. Add the vanilla extract and confectioners' sugar and beat together until smooth.

Spoon or pipe onto the tops of the cooled cupcakes and put a raspberry on top of each for decoration.

Enjoy!!

# ABOUT THE AUTHOR

Cindy Bell is a USA Today and Wall Street Journal Bestselling Author. She is the author of over one hundred books in twelve series. Her cozies are set in small towns, with lovable animals, quirky characters, delicious food and a touch of romance. She loves writing twisty cozy mysteries that keep readers guessing until the end.

When she is not reading or writing, she loves baking (and eating) sweet treats or walking along the beach with Rufus, her energetic Cocker Spaniel, thinking of the next adventure her characters can embark on.

You can find out more about Cindy's books at www.cindybellbooks.com.

ALSO BY CINDY BELL

MADDIE MILLS COZY MYSTERIES

Slain at the Sea

Homicide at the Harbor

Corpse at the Christmas Cookie Exchange

CHOCOLATE CENTERED COZY MYSTERIES

Chocolate Centered Cozy Mystery Series Box Set
(Books 1 - 4)

Chocolate Centered Cozy Mystery Series Box Set
(Books 5 - 8)

Chocolate Centered Cozy Mystery Series Box Set
(Books 9 - 12)

Chocolate Centered Cozy Mystery Series Box Set
(Books 13 - 16)

The Sweet Smell of Murder

A Deadly Delicious Delivery

A Bitter Sweet Murder

A Treacherous Tasty Trail

## SAGE GARDENS COZY MYSTERIES

## LITTLE LEAF CREEK COZY MYSTERY

## DUNE HOUSE COZY MYSTERIES

WAGGING TAIL COZY MYSTERIES

# NUTS ABOUT NUTS COZY MYSTERIES

A Tough Case to Crack

A Seed of Doubt

Roasted Peanuts and Peril

Chestnuts, Camping and Culprits

# DONUT TRUCK COZY MYSTERIES

Deadly Deals and Donuts

Fatal Festive Donuts

Bunny Donuts and a Body

Strawberry Donuts and Scandal

Frosted Donuts and Fatal Falls

# BEKKI THE BEAUTICIAN COZY MYSTERIES

Hairspray and Homicide

A Dyed Blonde and a Dead Body

Mascara and Murder

Pageant and Poison

Conditioner and a Corpse

Mistletoe, Makeup and Murder

Printed in Great Britain
by Amazon

86596693R00127